TARGET PRACTICE

Bert Drain and his two hired guns figured they had the drop on the Trailsman. They were dead wrong.

The one called Kenny pitched forward in midstride, sprawling along the ground followed by a trail of red. The other, shock in his face, emptied his gun. But he fired wildly as Fargo took aim. The man flew backward, perhaps three feet, before he went onto his back, kicked for a moment, and then lay still.

Bert Drain let his gun fall to the ground, terror in the grayness of his face. "No, Jesus, no," he begged.

"This is your lucky day. I'm going to let you live," Fargo said.

The Trailsman was saving his bullets—for bigger game. . . .

THE TRAILSMAN

134

COUGAR DAWN

by

Jon Sharpe

A SIGNET BOOK

SIGNET
Published by the Penguin Group
Penguin Books USA Inc., 375 Hudson Street,
New York, New York 10014, U.S.A.
Penguin Books Ltd, 27 Wrights Lane,
London W8 5TZ, England
Penguin Books Australia Ltd, Ringwood,
Victoria, Australia
Penguin Books Canada Ltd, 10 Alcorn Avenue,
Toronto, Ontario, Canada M4V 3B2
Penguin Books (N.Z.) Ltd, 182-190 Wairau Road,
Auckland 10, New Zealand

Penguin Books Ltd, Registered Offices:
Harmondsworth, Middlesex, England

First published by Signet, an imprint of New American Library,
a division of Penguin Books USA Inc.

First Printing, February, 1993
10 9 8 7 6 5 4 3 2 1

The Trailsman

Beginnings . . . they bend the tree and they mark the man. Skye Fargo was born when he was eighteen. Terror was his midwife, vengeance his first cry. Killing spawned Skye Fargo, ruthless, cold-blooded murder. Out of the acrid smoke of gunpowder still hanging in the air, he rose, cried out a promise never forgotten.

The Trailsman they began to call him all across the West: searcher, scout, hunter, the man who could see where others only looked, his skills for hire but not his soul, the man who lived each day to the fullest, yet trailed each tomorrow. Skye Fargo, the Trailsman, the seeker who could take the wildness of a land and the wanting of a woman and make them his own.

1860, Lost Trail Pass in the Salmon River Mountains of the Idaho Territory, the wild land where death could strike by arrow, bullet, fang, or claw . . .

1

He had often thought about this moment, but her words said everything, better than he could. "I waited, wondered, never stopped hoping, Fargo," she said, and he nodded.

"Just couldn't get up this way till now," he said, his lake blue eyes taking in the young woman in front of him. Bonnie hadn't changed, not really, except for perhaps ten added pounds. Her medium brown hair and medium brown eyes were still part of an open, friendly face, more sweet than pretty, her smile still winsomely warm and direct. She seemed just as he last saw her those years ago, wearing a simple shirt, tan this time, and a black skirt. But he saw the moment of anger flare in her eyes.

"And you expect I'm so glad to see you I'll just jump right into bed with you," Bonnie said.

"No." Fargo laughed. "I don't expect that."

"Then you're wrong," she said and with one, quick motion pulled her buttons open and flung the shirt aside. Bonnie's breasts were still as he'd remembered, modest yet with enough fullness to fit perfectly on her average frame, average-size tips of average pink on modest pink circles. Everything about Bonnie was average except for her open, unvarnished honesty, her unwillingness to play games. That openness had always been part of her sweet attractiveness, and it was still so, he realized as her arms slid around his neck. His mouth pressed hers as she started to shed her clothes. He felt her skirt slide down as she pulled him with her onto the small but thick rug on the floor of her modest living room.

Bonnie's thighs, a little fleshier now, rose up at once to clasp around him as his hands roamed her body, and his lips found one modest breast. He sucked gently on the pink tip. "Yes, oh, God, Fargo . . . bring it back, bring it all back," she murmured, and her arms were around him, sliding up and down his back, and her convex little belly, also a little fuller, was already rising up for him. His hand slid down onto the very curly but small V and felt the firm softness just below the fibrous tendrils. He touched, felt her already moistened for him, and Bonnie gave her gasping half-scream and dug her fingers into his back. He pressed deeper, caressed the soft lips, touched the tender places and Bonnie's thighs opened and closed against him. "Oh God, yes . . . so good, so good," she moaned. "So wonderful . . . so good."

Her moans grew deeper and longer as he continued to caress and stroke, and when he brought his own pulsating warmth to her the moans changed into the tiny half-screamed gasps that came over and over and over as she pumped and rose with him, pushed and fell back with him, hurried moments, half-screams as much a plea to herself as to him until suddenly the half-screams grew in pitch and intensity, and he felt her pushing frantically against him. "Yes, yes, please, please, oh God, so long, so good, oh God," Bonnie flung out with her half-screams, and he let himself explode with her as his mouth bit gently into one modest breast, and Bonnie's soft thighs clasped tighter around his waist.

He stayed with her and let the world shatter with her. She prolonged the ecstasy as she slammed against him with her pelvis, harder and harder until, with a sudden cry, she fell back. But her arms stayed clutched around his neck, holding his mouth against her breasts. "Oh Jesus, oh, God," she murmured into his cheek. "So good, so great, just the way it was, the way I remembered." Her hands came against the sides of his face. "It was always special with you, Fargo, always special."

"And you still don't play games." He smiled.

"No, not with you," she said.

"Not with anyone, I'll wager," he said, and her smile was almost rueful.

"That's true. I can't. It's not part of me. I do or I don't. I will or I won't," she said. "It's been mostly won't, but I'm sure you realized that."

"I wish I could stay longer," he said.

"I'll have to make whatever time we have last me till next time," Bonnie said, and she curled herself tight against him. He heard the sound of her steady breathing in minutes. She always slept soundly as a baby afterward, he remembered, and woke up hungry for more. He lay back, cradled her against him as he smiled. It was always nice when memories held up to time. He found himself thinking of the last time he had lain like this with Bonnie.

Because of her open, honest sweetness, he had already developed a special fondness for her. She was trying to make a small dry-goods store pay in a grubby little town in Utah while fighting off the advances of Banker Jethroe, the most powerful man in town. That night flooded back over him as vividly as if it had been yesterday. He was sliding from Bonnie's sleeping form in the big bed to go into the kitchen and draw some water. He walked silently on bare feet, his powerful body naked in the dim light of a kitchen candle. He was drinking deeply of the water when he heard the front door burst open, and when he rushed into Bonnie's room, the heavy figure of Banker Jethroe was already on top of her, punching her as he pushed her legs open.

Fargo moved with long, silent strides and yanked the man up, flung him halfway across the room, and Banker Jethroe's heavy figure crashed on the floor. The man pushed to his feet, mean and drunk, Fargo saw, his heavy-featured face flushed. He rushed, drew one arm back to swing, and Fargo's whistling left hook caught him on the side of the jaw. He staggered backward, fell, shook his head, and looked up as his eyes cleared. "She's through in this town, mister," the man said as he rose. "She's through and you're dead."

"Get out before I break you in little pieces," Fargo said. Out of the corner of his eye he saw that Bonnie had flung her robe on and rushed to a dresser against the far wall. Banker Jethroe came at him again, his words thick-tongued.

"Let's see you do it," he snarled, and Fargo cursed silently as he took a step forward, his hands ready to lash out when the man yanked the gun from his pocket, a Sharps four-barreled derringer, a deadly weapon at close range, with the rotating striker on the hammer firing the barrels in rotation. Fargo halted, suddenly aware of his nakedness. He saw Jethroe's finger tightening on the trigger, winced, and the room exploded with the shot, far too loud for the derringer. His glance snapped to Bonnie and saw the big Remington-Beals with its seven-inch barrel in her hands.

Banker Jethroe lay on the floor, his heavy midsection suddenly turned red, and Fargo stepped past the man and took the revolver from Bonnie's hands.

"Oh, God, what do we do?" she breathed.

"Get dressed," Fargo said as he started to pull on clothes.

"There's no hiding this. He's a prominent man," Bonnie said, staring at the lifeless figure.

"*Was* a prominent man," Fargo said, putting the revolver atop the dresser. "Everyone knows he was bothering you. You told me that." Bonnie nodded. "He burst in, found us together, and tried to kill you. I had to shoot him."

"You? No, I did it. I'll say so," Bonnie said, and he took her by the shoulders and turned her to face him.

"You have to go on living in this town. I don't. I'll go my way. I shot him. We'll leave it like that," he told her. "I'll go fetch the sheriff, and he can clear this formerly prominent man out of your bedroom."

"I won't let you take the blame for me," Bonnie said.

"Self-defense. It'll be our word against his, and he won't be saying much," Fargo said. "You stay just the way you are till I get back." He hurried from the small house, found the sheriff's office, and woke the man up in his living quarters in the back. He told the sheriff the story he and Bonnie had agreed upon as he walked with the man to Bonnie's place.

"Self-defense, you say," the sheriff muttered.

"That's right," Fargo nodded and saw the sheriff wince. "Something wrong with that?" Fargo asked.

"Plenty," the sheriff said. "I've always liked Bonnie. I'm real sorry about this, but Banker Jethroe was an important man in town. He may be dead, but his influence isn't.''

"Meaning what exactly?" Fargo asked, peering hard at the sheriff. He seemed a man who was honestly pained for Bonnie.

"We'll go into that later," the sheriff said. "But enough folks heard Bonnie say she'd kill Jethroe if he kept bothering her."

"Damn," Fargo swore softly.

"Exactly," the sheriff said.

"But I'm the one who shot him. He was going to kill me," Fargo said.

"You can tell your story when the time comes," the sheriff said. Fargo swore again, silently this time as they reached Bonnie's house and entered. Bonnie sat at the edge of the bed and rose as Fargo stepped into the room with the sheriff. "Hello, Bonnie," the sheriff said quietly. "Your friend here told me what happened. You'd be backing up his story, I take it." "Yes," Bonnie said, swallowing, and the sheriff gazed down at the still figure of Banker Jethroe, then turned to Fargo and put his hand on the Colt in Fargo's holster. Fargo's fingers closed around the man's wrist instantly. "I'd like a look at your gun, mister," the sheriff said calmly and waited, his eyes meeting Fargo's gaze. " 'Less you've some reason why I shouldn't," he said.

Fargo grimaced inwardly as he realized that to refuse would be an admission. He unclasped his fingers and the sheriff drew the Colt, spun the chamber, and his eyes narrowed. "Six-shot revolver, six bullets in it," he said, raised the barrel of the gun to his nose, and sniffed. "This gun hasn't been fired in the last twenty minutes," he said and stepped back, his eyes sweeping the room to halt at the pistol atop the dresser. He stepped to it, flipped the chamber open, and his face took on a pained grimace as he turned to Bonnie. "Want to tell me anything, girl?" he asked.

"I didn't say I shot him with *my* gun," Fargo put in quickly.

"I shot him," Bonnie said quietly, and her eyes went to Fargo. "I won't let you take the blame for it," she said.

"Dammit, Bonnie," Fargo said.

"He was going to kill Fargo," Bonnie said. "He had the derringer pointed right at him."

"Under the law, that doesn't make it self-defense for you, Bonnie," the sheriff said.

"She came to my defense," Fargo said. "He was going to attack her."

"That'll be up to a jury to decide," the sheriff said. "You dress, Bonnie. I'll wait outside. I have to take you in." He motioned to Fargo, who stepped from the house with him.

"There's no reason for her to sit in jail," Fargo said.

"Can't let her stay free. Got to protect my job," the man said. "Remember what I said about Banker Jethroe's influence still being alive? A jury we call will be made up of townsfolk, and the bank holds loans and mortgages on most everybody who'll sit on that jury. The rest of the bank's trustees won't take kindly to a jury letting go the woman that killed their president. They could call in every note and loan, and everybody will know that."

"You're saying they'll feel they have to convict her," Fargo said with a frown.

"I'm telling you the facts of human nature, mister," the sheriff said. "I know Jethroe was a bastard, but what I know won't count."

"Thanks for being honest," Fargo said as Bonnie

15

came from the house. He walked in silence beside her to the jail, two small cells alongside the sheriff's office with a guard sitting in an outside room.

"Cell one," the sheriff told the guard who ushered Bonnie into the first small cell. She offered Fargo a wan smile as he cursed silently.

"I'll be by in the morning," he told her and walked outside with the sheriff.

"You can visit her any time you like," the sheriff said. "Early morning, late night, whenever you want." Fargo's eyes peered at the sheriff. The man's face showed no emotion, yet Fargo had the distinct feeling he was doing more than spelling out visiting hours.

"What if they convict her, and she escapes?" Fargo asked the man.

"I'd have to send out wanted flyers for her as an escaped murderess," the sheriff said. "Of course, if she escaped before a trial she'd only be wanted for questioning. I wouldn't be sending out fliers for that."

Fargo forced himself not to smile as he adopted the sheriff's bland demeanor. "Naturally. No conviction, she can't be wanted for a crime," he said.

"Naturally." The sheriff nodded.

"See you around," Fargo said as he strode off. He took the Ovaro, spent the night bedded down outside of town, and paid his first visit to Bonnie in the morning. "You can't stay. It could go badly," he told her in a whispered exchange.

"Doesn't seem I've much choice," she said.

"More than you think. What would you be taking with you if you were leaving here?" he asked.

"My clothes and my money," Bonnie said.

"The money in the bank?"

"No. I took it out. I couldn't stand going there anymore and having to see Jethroe every time. It's buried under the floor in the kitchen," Bonnie told him.

"I'll be back tonight," he said. She was frowning when he left, the unsaid things racing through her mind, and it was late that night when he returned. She stood at the bars, no frown this time, but a tiny smile edging her lips. She watched in silence as he took the guard's gun and tied the man up securely, then let her out of the cell. "I've all your things and a horse out back," he said. "Where do we go?"

"North, I've some friends in Wyoming. They'll help me get started again," she said.

"North it is," he said.

The pictures snapped off in his mind, and he looked at Bonnie's form beside him, still asleep in his arms. Her friends had taken her in, and from there she'd found her way to the place she was now. She'd reached him by post with that news, the last letter over a year ago, and he found her as content as she'd sounded then. The job, taking care of the books for a small gold mining operation, seemed to be to her liking, and he was happy for her. Bonnie deserved a run of happiness. Not because she'd saved his life once, but because she was basically a good person.

He smiled down at her as she stirred and opened her eyes, and he saw the instant message in them. Her mouth came up to press against his, the message given tangible form, and almost at once she was pressing one soft, modest breast to his lips. The night grew warm again with her flesh and her hungering desire, and he was spent and more than satisfied when she curled up against him once again, her last, lingering scream of pleasure still hanging in the air. Later, when the dawn woke them both, she brought him a mug of coffee and sat cross-legged on the bed beside him, the tan shirt hardly concealing her soft-fleshed body.

"Tell me about this boss of yours, this Jim Gibson. He was so damn excited when I showed up looking for you," Fargo said.

"Yes, I'm sure he was. You've a reputation, you know, Fargo," Bonnie reminded him.

"He said he had to talk to me, and I told him not till I'd seen you. I know he'll be waiting come sunup," Fargo said.

"Jim Gibson is a strong man. He runs his mine with a strong hand. But he's fair. I've seen that," Bonnie said. "Then he had a real tragedy a few months back. It's changed him, made him harder, more obsessed. I know that's what he wants to talk to you about."

"Go on," Fargo said as she paused.

"I'd rather he tell you," Bonnie said. "Listen to him. I hope you can help him. He'll pay you anything you ask, I'm sure."

Fargo made a face. "I've a job waiting; Bill Bannister in Montana wants me to trailblaze a herd for him," he said. "I'd stay longer with you, otherwise."

"Hear him out. I'm sure, when he saw you, it was better than finding a new strike for him," Bonnie said.

"I'll listen, for you," Fargo said and received a long, slow kiss for his answer.

"Can you stay another night?" Bonnie asked, and he nodded. Bonnie swung happily from the bed, the shirt flying up to show her very round little rear. "See you then," she said, hurrying off to bathe and dress. He lay in the bed, waiting for her to finish. When he heard her leave, he rose, bathed, and pulled on his clothes and stepped from the little house. The mine stretched out in front of him: the low-roofed wooden building that was the office a hundred yards on, and beyond it the wooden sluices and long toms that ran down from the dark entrances of the caves. He strolled across the ground to the office building, glanced in a window, and saw Bonnie at work in a small office, two heavy ledger books in front of her on a table.

Jim Gibson greeted him as he entered and took him into another room with two chairs and a table. "Been waiting. Bonnie told me you'd be coming by," Gibson said. He had a square face, graying hair, Fargo took note, a strong, lined face, and the eyes of a man who had met the world and won, most of the time. In Gibson's dark blue orbs he saw the pain of bitterness. "Bonnie told me about you over the last few years, how you two had a special relationship," the man said. "And how she'd given up that you'd ever get this way."

"Finally managed it," Fargo smiled.

"Thank God," Jim Gibson said fervently. "You'll be my last hope. And the best one."

"For what?"

"For finding my son, Josh," Gibson said.

"He's lost?"

"It's not as simple as that," Jim Gibson said and gestured to a chair as he paced the small room. "Josh was not only my son, he was my partner and my right hand. It was his idea, and it was working until something went wrong."

"Whoa. Back up some," Fargo said.

"Yes, I'm sorry," Gibson said and drew a deep breath before he began again. "The main road north circles around to Missoula. It's a damn magnet for every band of thievin' gunslingers. They hit stages, payroll wagons, gold shipments, mail riders, everything and anything. We kept losing our gold shipments

19

until Josh got this idea. He'd take the gold in saddlebags, alone, through the mountains. No varmints would look for a man riding alone through the mountains with nothing to draw attention to him. It worked, over and over. I'd send dummy shipments they'd attack and go off cussing while Josh would be taking the gold through the mountains, the heart of the Bitterroot Range."

"But something went wrong," Fargo offered.

"He never came back from his last trip."

"They caught on and dry gulched him?"

"No, we'd have found him then. Besides, at the time he disappeared they had attacked three stages on the main road. Something happened to Josh, but they didn't do it. I can't go on without knowing what happened to him or whether he's still alive. I don't sleep maybe three hours a night.

"When did he disappear?" Fargo asked.

"Two months ago."

"Two months is a very cold trail." Fargo frowned.

"I know you've done colder," Jim Gibson said.

"What makes you think he might still be alive?" Fargo questioned.

"I don't know, but there was a man came to me, Roy Coulter. He lives in the mountains and said he knew what happened to Josh. He wouldn't say if Josh was alive. He wouldn't say anything more unless I paid him. I decided he was just trying to get money out of me and he didn't know anything. I refused to pay him, and he left. Later, I wondered if I'd made a mistake about Roy Coulter, and I went searching for him."

"You didn't find him," Fargo said.

"No, but those damn mountains are made for hiding," Gibson said. "I tried to get the army to help me."

"The army?" Fargo frowned.

"They have a small garrison at the foot of the Beaverhead range where some families have settled in. They were useless. They didn't even do much looking," the man said darkly.

"I'm sorry for what's happened, but I'm afraid I can't help. I'm due in Montana to trailblaze a new route. It's a deal all settled months ago," Fargo said.

"I'll pay you triple what they will," Gibson said.

"Sorry. I don't go back on my word," Fargo said. "I can't help you."

"You're my last hope, a chance I never thought I'd get. You're the Trailsman. I can't just let you ride away without trying to find Josh," the man said with a mixture of steel and pleading in his voice.

"God knows how long this would take. I don't have time enough. They're expecting me in Montana. I'm real sorry but the cards just don't fall right. Maybe, when I'm finished in Montana I could swing by this way again," Fargo said.

"The trail will be even colder then, and I might be dead from exhaustion," Gibson bit out.

"It's the best I can do. I'm sorry," Fargo said.

"Goddammit," Gibson said, slamming his fist onto the table in an explosion of anger and frustration. "It's not fair, not one goddamn bit fair. You're here, and you're my last chance. Not fair, dammit, not fair."

"Didn't say it was. Not a hell of a lot in life is fair," Fargo said, getting to his feet. "Sorry, again," he said as he left. He felt the man's eyes boring into his back as he went out the door. He felt sorry for Jim Gibson, a man plainly distraught and at the end of his tether. There was some time before he was due at Bill Bannister's, Fargo knew, but not enough for this kind of searching a cold trail. He shook away the bitterness in the man's eyes, took the Ovaro, and led the horse behind Bonnie's place, where he spent the rest of the day giving the animal a thorough currying, using the sweat-scraper first, then the body brush and sponge for its eyes, nostrils, and lips, and lastly the stable rubber.

When he finished, the day was drawing to an end and the Ovaro gleamed and glistened, jet fore- and hindquarters stark against the pure white midsection. Bonnie returned, had a stew on the kettle, and he ate with her. "You're awfully quiet," he observed.

"I was hoping you'd help Jim Gibson," she said.

"I told you I was due in Montana," he reminded her. "You said to hear him out, and I did."

"I know," Bonnie nodded unhappily. "I just hoped. He's so desperate and he's changed so, grown harsh and bitter, driving his men unmercifully. Everyone's aware of it."

"That's something he'll have to work out on his own," Fargo shrugged. Bonnie nodded again, cleared away the dishes, and led him into the bedroom where she quickly excluded the rest of the world. It was only after her cries of pleasure had died away for the second time that she allowed the world to intrude. "You'll be leaving come morning, won't you?" she murmured.

"That's right," he said. "Maybe I can swing back this way when I'm finished."

"I won't wait. I won't think about it, either," she said matter-of-factly. "That only makes waiting harder." He held her against him and understood, and she slept tight in his arms. When morning came, he slid from beside her, dressed, and paused at the door to glance back at her. She lay unmoving, apparently still fast asleep, but he wondered as he left and promised he'd try to return when the Bannister job was finished.

He took the Ovaro and set off leisurely across the low hills along the south end of the Beaverhead range. He had been riding for a little over an hour when he spotted the four horsemen coming at a full gallop behind him. He continued on as he watched them draw closer, and he reined to a halt at a small plateau bordered by a stand of dwarf maple and waited. The four riders reached him in minutes and pulled their mounts to a stop. "Jim Gibson sent us," the one man said. He was middle-aged with a tired face. The other three were ordinary enough, a little younger, Fargo noted, one sporting a thin mustache. "We've orders to bring you back," the older man said.

"I said all I had to say," Fargo replied. "There's no point in my going back."

The older man sounded apologetic. "We've our orders. We don't want trouble," he said.

"Me neither, so's you just go back and tell him I said I wouldn't go with you," Fargo suggested.

The man made a face. "We can't do that. He told us to bring you back the hard way if we had to."

"Then that's what you're going to have to do, gents," Fargo smiled.

2

His smile stayed as he saw them draw their guns. "Now, you know and I know you won't be using them. Gibson doesn't want me back dead," he said.

"Damn," the older man said as he pushed his gun back into its holster. "Get him," he snapped, and the other three men moved their horses forward. Fargo spurred the pinto hard, and the horse reared, forelegs striking out, and two of the others pulled their mounts away at once. The pinto came down, and Fargo sent the horse racing forward directly at the older man who tried to twist away. He didn't move quickly enough, and Fargo's left hand smashed into the side of his face, and he toppled from his horse. Fargo kept the Ovaro racing forward and had almost reached the edge of the dwarf maples when he felt the lariat drop around his shoulders.

"Damn," he swore, the one move he hadn't expected. He felt the rope tighten around him, and he leaped before he was yanked from the saddle. He landed on the ground on both feet, grabbed hold of the rope around him, and pulled with all his strength. But the rider had been smart enough and quick enough to wrap the lariat around his saddle horn, and Fargo felt himself yanked from his feet. He hit the ground, still clinging to the lariat with both hands as he was pulled along the ground until the rider halted and leaped from his horse. On his knees, Fargo saw the man come toward him, and he glimpsed the others dismounting to join him. As the man reached him, Fargo swung both hands at once in an upward arc, slammed his fists into the man's midsection, and the figure bent double as he staggered backward.

Fargo saw two of the others rushing at him, and instead of getting to his feet and taking their blows, he dived, flung himself forward, and they collided with each other as they rushed at him. He twisted, hit the ground on his back, and kicked upward with both legs. One of the two cursed in pain as the double blow slammed into his knee. He went down and Fargo rolled, the other man's kick just grazing his face. He rolled again, gained thirty seconds that let him tear the lariat from around his shoulders as the man charged him. Again, he ducked low, and the man's first blow went over his head and Fargo twisted aside and sunk a short right to the man's stomach, taking the moment to get his feet in balance. The man rushed at him again, and Fargo parried his first blow, bringing up a whistling left hook that landed flush on the man's jaw.

Fargo spun as the man went down. Then he saw the older man and the one with the thin mustache coming at him. They charged in bull-like rushes, and Fargo danced away from both, feinting at the older man with a left and giving the second one a chance to rush at him from the side. But he had almost planned the man's move, and he was ready and waiting. He sidestepped the first rush, parried a wild wing right, and crossed his own left hook under it. The blow caught the man on the point of the jaw, and he went down, and Fargo spun just in time to duck under the older man's straight-arm punch. He brought up his own uppercut up in a tremendous blow, and the man's head snapped back, and he almost somersaulted backward as he hit the ground.

The thin-mustached one had regained his feet but he was still wobbly, trying to clear his head, when Fargo pulled the big Colt and smashed the butt on the man's head. Fargo saw the other two getting to their feet as the mustached one collapsed in a heap. He leaped forward, swung the Colt sideways, and slammed into the one man's temple, and the man crumpled. The fourth one saw the gun in Fargo's hand, backed away and, plainly deciding the rules had changed, went for his gun. Fargo let him clear his holster before he fired, and the man cursed in pain as his six-gun flew from his hand.

"That's enough," Fargo said and stepped forward as the man held his numbed hand against his waist. "Lay down on your face," he ordered, and the man obeyed.

"Christ, my hand," the man complained.

"It'll be fine in a few days. My shot hit the gun," Fargo said as he strode to one of their horses and took the lariat from from its saddle strap. He cast a quick glance at the other three. Two were still unconscious, and one was groaning. As he started to come around, Fargo tied the wrists of the nearest one first, then the others, until he had all four bound. He perched on a log as they regained full consciousness, then had them climb onto their horses, and tied another length of lariat from each man to the next. Finally, he climbed onto the Ovaro and led his captives behind him single file as he slowly road back to Gibson's mine.

Gibson came out of his office as Fargo halted outside and dropped the end of the lariat to the ground.

"I'm back, but only to tell you not to send anyone else. I might get real irritated next time," Fargo said.

"I didn't know how else to get you back. I've got to find out about Josh. You're the best chance I'll ever have for that," Gibson said.

"I heard you the first time," Fargo said. "Don't make the same mistake twice."

"Talk to Bonnie. She's at her place," the man said.

"Bonnie's not going to change my mind any," Fargo said.

"Go talk to her anyway," Gibson insisted, and Fargo shot him a probing glance. The man's face was impassive, and Fargo walked the Ovaro across the ground to Bonnie's hut, dismounted, and pushed the half-ajar door open.

"Bonnie?" he called, and only silence answered. He stepped into the room, saw it was empty, and then his eyes halted at the folded piece of notepaper propped against the lamp. He picked it up, and the frown slid across his brow as he read.

Fargo . . .
　Try and help him. I don't think he'd hurt me, but I can't be sure. I think this has all driven him a little crazy. Seems we're turning back the clock in more ways than one.
　Whatever you do, I'll understand.
　　　　　　　　　　　Love . . . Bonnie.

Fargo crumpled the note in one hand as he stormed from the hut, and he strode into Gibson's office. "Let her go, goddammit," he spit out as Gibson faced him.

"I can't, not until I know about Josh," the man said.

Fargo drew the Colt, his voice as cold as the steel of the barrel of the gun. "All you'll know about is being dead," he growled.

"I took her after you left. I'm the only one who knows where she is. Kill me and you kill her," Gibson said.

"Goddamn you," Fargo said, and Gibson's smile was made of wry ruefulness.

"Desperation makes a man clever, Fargo," Gibson said. Fargo swore silently and knew the truth in the words. "Look, I don't want to hurt her. She's safe. When you come back, she goes free, keeps her job, and gets a raise. All I want is for you to find Josh for me."

Fargo's lips stayed grim as he dropped the Colt back in its holster. Jim Gibson was very much a man on the edge, made of desperate unpredictability. He could snap if one more door was slammed in his face. The fingers of Fargo's left hand unclasped, and Bonnie's note uncrumpled. But the words stayed imprinted inside him, one line swimming into his mind: *turning back the clock in more ways than one.* "Maybe I can't find him. Maybe I won't find anything," Fargo said to the man.

"You try, that's what I want. You try, Fargo. You're the best. You come back and tell me you tried," the man said, and Fargo drew a deep breath as he let himself slump into a chair.

"All right, it's a deal. But if anything happens to Bonnie, you're a dead man," Fargo said.

"I know that," Gibson nodded as he sat down.

"Tell me everything, what route he usually took, what kind of horse he rode, his clothes, everything about him," Fargo said.

"He took his own ways, different every time," Gibson said. "But he always went through Lost Trail Pass as a starting place. He liked gray clothes, wore gray shirts, and gray jeans and a gray hat. He rode a quarter horse, mostly sorrel with a sprinkling of white. But Josh had one indulgence. He loved fancy saddles, and the one he used mostly had a hand-stitched cantle with fancy designs cut into the leather and a silver horn."

"That gives me a little," Fargo said as he rose.

Gibson pulled a roll of bills from his pocket and handed them to Fargo. "Payment in advance. You're an honest man, I'm sure. Find my boy, Fargo. Find him or find out what happened to him. I'll take it from there."

"You see to Bonnie," Fargo said as he left the office and returned to the pinto. The day was more than half over, and he turned north on the fairly flat land that bordered the Beaverhead range. He found a place to bed down beneath a cluster of juniper, laid out his bedroll, and undressed to his underwear, the Colt at his side. The night stayed warm, and he listened to the sound of foxes squabbling, the distant call of a timber wolf, and the scurrying of racoons and martens nearby. A half-moon offered pale light, but the distant mountains rose high, a black bulk that seemed to signal the end of the earth. Fargo thought about the cushion of time he'd allowed before he was due at Bill Bannister's. It had seemed more than enough, and now it seemed not nearly enough, and he swore at the workings of fate as he drew sleep around himself.

When morning's bright sun woke him, he found a stream in which to wash and refill his canteen and a cluster of wild plums on which to breakfast. He continued on northward. The towering mountains in the distance seemed to reach the sky, all part of the Bitterroot range that ran north to south. Each group had its own name: the Sapphire Mountains, the Beaver-head range, the Cabinet Mountains, the Lost River range, all heavily forested and lush with game, all embracing beauty and sudden death to any intruder.

This was Nez Percé land, along with the Northern Shoshoni and sometimes the Blackfoot coming down from the north and the Crow up from the south. But mostly it was the Northern Shoshoni and Nez Percé arrows one had to dodge, and he rode carefully as he moved into the low hills. There was still plenty of open space, and the trees mostly hackberry, haw-thorn, and juniper. He had been well into the late morning when he saw the line of horsemen appear ahead and slightly below, riding in a column of pairs, their dark blue uniforms with gold kerchiefs identifying them without the platoon pennant one trooper carried. Fargo nudged the Ovaro downward, and the column drew to a halt. He counted ten troopers and a lieutenant at the head, a young-faced officer with sandy hair poking from beneath his hat.

"Which way are you riding, mister?" the lieutenant asked.

"North, into mountain country," Fargo said.

"I'd ride back to the base with us. The Northern Shoshoni are out riding and raiding again. We just found the Thompkins family massacred in their home," the officer said. "That's the third family in the past month. It's terrible, real terrible. God, they're all torn up."

"Where?" Fargo asked grimly.

"Turn right over the next hill. The Thompkins place is up along the high land, a line of hackberry just behind it. The damn savages must've come out of the trees and surprised all of them," the lieutenant said, his face showing both fear and disgust.

"I'll go have a look," Fargo said.

"We can take you, if you want," the officer offered.

"I'll find it. I'll smell it," Fargo said.

"Smell it?" The lieutenant frowned.

"The smell of burned wood lasts a long time, for days, usually," Fargo said.

"They didn't torch the place. Didn't touch anything, in fact, except mutilate and kill the Thompkins," the officer said.

"That's strange, not like them," Fargo said. "Where's your garrison?"

"North about ten miles. Captain Osgood's in command. It's a small garrison, and we're supposed to patrol a lot of territory where the settlers have put up their places,"

"You saying too much territory and too few men?" Fargo half smiled.

"Guess I am," the young officer said, and Fargo let his smile broaden. It was a familiar enough complaint in the army, but in this instance perhaps a valid one.

"I'll stop by at the post later," he said and drew a salute as the lieutenant sent his column southward at a trot. Fargo rode on, followed the officer's instructions, and turned west when he crossed the hill. He saw the cabin set on a slight rise of land, pigpens spreading out from both sides of it, and he dismounted when he reached the scene. Three bodies lay strewn across the front yard—a man and two children—and then he saw the woman's body just in front of the open door of the house. A long-barreled plains rifle lay on the ground half across her ankles. She'd clearly come out with the rifle and never had the chance to fire it.

Fargo knelt down beside the man first. He hadn't been scalped, but his face had been ripped off, and very viciously. The man's abdomen lay exposed, his intestines spilled out, the kind of slash a hunting knife could have inflicted. Fargo rose and stepped to the bodies of the two children. Both their necks were torn open, and the young girl had slash marks down the length of her body that had shredded her cotton dress. He went to the woman and squatted down beside her. A slashing hole extended from the base of her neck to her exposed left breast, where the top had been torn off. The bottom of her long muslin dress had been ripped away, and her belly bore a half-dozen deep cuts that were still running red. He rose and stepped into the house, swept the room with a quick glance, and walked into an adjoining room, which was the bedroom. There were two trundle beds and a puncheon bed against one wall. He saw an old dresser with jewelry lying atop it, pins and beads and two hand mirrors. Nothing had been touched, nothing disturbed, and his forehead wore a furrow as he left the house.

He climbed onto the Ovaro and slowly walked the horse from the front yard of the house. The army would send a burial party and a chaplain in the morning, after the lieutenant reported back. That was the usual way of things, and Fargo halted, let his eyes scan the ground in front of the house, turned, and slowly rode to the edge of the hackberry and again scanned the ground. The furrow stayed on his forehead as he finally rode away with the sun sliding down over the distant mountain tops. Following the lieutenant's directions, he found the army post soon after night embraced the land, the twinkling of lamplight and the odor of campfire leading him the last quarter mile.

The post was indeed a sparse one, he saw as he

drew to a halt. There was a long stable of stout logs, and opposite it the barracks building. A company pennant drooped in the windless night atop a small, separate building. The post hadn't more than thirty-five men, he guessed, counting cooks and chaplain, definitely an army outpost camp. Two sentries appeared as he rode into the post grounds. " 'Evening," he said. "Name's Fargo, Skye Fargo. Met one of your patrols this afternoon. The lieutenant invited me to stop by." The two sentries nodded and stepped back as he walked the horse forward. "Captain Osgood?" he asked.

"Building with the company pennant," one of the soldiers said, and Fargo walked to the small building, dismounted, and knocked on the door.

"Come in," a voice answered, and he opened the door and made his way into a neat office where a curtain closed off the entranceway to living quarters. The officer behind a small desk wore a crisp uniform and a young face, dark-haired with a straight nose and dark eyes that regarded him with polite friendliness.

"Met one of your patrols a little while back," Fargo began.

"Yes, Lieutenant Andrews mentioned it to me, right after they found the Thompkins place," the officer said. "I'm Captain Osgood."

"Skye Fargo."

"Andrews said you were going to go on for a look at the Thompkins place. Brutal, wasn't it? Andrews was sick over it," the captain said. "The damn Northern Shoshoni are getting more and more vicious."

"It wasn't the Northern Shoshoni. Not the Nez Percé, either," Fargo said. "It wasn't any Indian."

"What do you mean?" Captain Osgood frowned.

"I've seen Indian raids from one part of the country

33

to the other. Never saw one like this. Indians on a rampage don't just kill. They steal, take whatever they fancy or they feel they can use, and then they burn and destroy what's left. The Thompkins place wasn't burned down, and the woman had jewelry on a dresser that wasn't even touched, the kind of thing Indians almost always take," Fargo said. "Believe me, I know Indians, Captain."

"I believe you. All I know about Indians is what I've learned since they sent me out here. It's not much, and I don't like any of it," the captain said. He was honest, sincere, Fargo saw at once, not afraid to admit what he didn't know. And it was plain he was more than a little fearful.

"Were the other two families ripped and torn the same way?" Fargo asked.

"Pretty much the same," the captain said.

"Not the Northern Shoshoni," Fargo mused aloud.

"Then what? Some madman with a sickle or bayonet?" Osgood retorted.

"Maybe, but I'd say an animal, probably a cougar from the wounds I saw," Fargo said.

"A cougar? But they don't pick out people to attack, unless some trapper comes onto their lair," Captain Osgood said.

"That's right. Not usually. But then neither do grizzlies unless they suddenly change their normal habits. Yet you've heard of rogue bears. That can happen with any animal," Fargo said and watched the captain's young face darken in thought.

"The mountains are full of cougars, and they do wander down sometimes," he murmured.

"Humans are easy pickings for the mountain lion that develops a taste and a habit," Fargo remarked.

"Good God, we've got our problems with the Shoshoni. How can we protect them from a damn cougar that steals down like the wind?" the captain said.

"Tell the others to be on guard against more than the Shoshoni," Fargo said. "Now I want some information from you. What can you tell me about a man named Josh Gibson?"

"Not much. His father visited us, and we had our patrols look for any sign of him for a while, but we didn't find anything. But he was high into the mountains, and we don't go up there. I told that to Jim Gibson. He wasn't happy with us," the captain said.

"What about a man named Roy Coulter?"

"We keep hearing stories about him, but we've never seen him. Some say he's mad, kind of a wild recluse. All I can tell you is that he's around up in the mountains," Osgood said. "Truth is, we've all we can do to keep our patrols along this area."

Fargo nodded and felt a twinge of sympathy for Osgood, a young officer dumped in a place beyond his experience or abilities. But then that wasn't unusual for the army, he realized. "Anything you can tell me at all?" he asked.

"There's a kind of town just below Lost Trail Pass. They call it Last Chance. Mostly it's an inn and stable and a trading post, all run by a man named Bert Drain. A barber who's drunk most of the time has a store, and a one-armed blacksmith has a shop. Prospectors and trappers heading into the high mountains stop there from time to time. You might pick up a lead there."

"Much obliged, Captain," Fargo said, exchanged a handshake, and left the captain's office. He rode from the post grounds, went perhaps a mile north, and bedded down beside a bur oak. He watched the moon travel slowly across the sky and disappear behind the tall peaks as he went to sleep. When morning came he woke and took a long moment to gaze up at the forbidding walls of thick greenery with their rock spires that seemed to almost poke the sky. These towering mountains were keepers of their own secrets, implacable guardians of all that took place within their fastness. Did they hold the secret of Josh Gibson's disappearance, he wondered. And if they did, could he pry it loose from their silence?

He dressed and sent the Ovaro north again. This time the terrain climbed sharply with steep slopes, and then there were stretches of high plateaus. He scanned the ground as he rode, mountain brush with lots of dogbane and peppergrass. The unshod prints of Indian ponies were plentiful, their trails crisscrossing one another. He found two broken arrows against the trunk of an oak, shafts that had plainly been aimed at a deer and had missed their mark. He picked the pieces up and examined the markings at the tail ends of the shafts. "Northern Shoshoni," he grunted aloud as he rode on. He had gone into the early afternoon when he drew to a halt as he spied the line of near-naked horsemen. He backed into a cluster of bur oak and watched the redmen pass nearby, six, he counted, a hunting party. He had no need to see markings to know they were Northern Shoshoni. That was plain in the finer-featured planes of their faces. The Northern Shoshoni were a handsomer race than most Indian tribes and more pure-blooded than most, outranked in purity only by the Cheyenne, Ute, and Arapaho out of some thirty plains tribes.

They rode casually and confidently, Fargo noted, and he let them pass out of sight before he emerged from the trees to move on. But a small hunting party meant that there had to be at least a trail camp not too far away, and he rode the steep trails with added caution. Time was important in trailing the path of Josh Gibson. He wanted to stay clear of the kind of problems the Shoshoni could bring. The terrain grew steeper, and he was glad for the places where it leveled off. The day was starting to slide to an end when he reached the spot just south of Lost Trail Pass, the ramshackle collection of buildings very much as the captain had described them.

The sturdiest was the center one that bore the name of Last Chance Inn, a stable attached to the rear. The trading post occupied a structure a few feet to the right, and three more flat-roofed buildings spread out from the inn. Fargo halted, and as he swung to the ground a man stepped from the trading post. Fargo took in a medium figure, a hint of burliness to it, a heavy-cheeked face with a flat nose and a mouth that turned down at the corners. Watery but shrewd eyes appraised him at once. Two men followed him outside, both wearing cartridge belts across their chests, both walking with a swagger. They halted a few paces behind the first man. "Bert Drain," the man said. "Fine-looking animal you've got there."

"He is," Fargo said. "Name's Fargo. I'm looking for a room for the night."

"You've got one," Bert Drain said. Fargo smiled inwardly as he saw the man's eyes flick to the Ovaro again. He gave it a quick examination as he looked for miner's equipment or trapper's gear. "What brings you into the mountains, mister?" the man asked.

"Looking to see if there's an easy mail route through the range," Fargo said, drawing a curt snort from Bert Drain.

"There's no easy route to anywhere but hell through those mountains, Fargo," the man said. "Right, boys?"

37

he added, glancing back at the two men, who both nodded. Only their lips smiled, Fargo noted. "Kenny and Carl, my bodyguards," Drain said.

Fargo let one eyebrow lift. "Bodyguards?" he queried.

"This is a lonely place. I've a lot of stuff in my store. I don't want anyone getting ideas. Then there are the damn Indians. With Kenny and Carl I sleep sound. They're crack shots," Drain said, a mixture of bragging and warning coloring his tone.

"That's nice," Fargo said with a smile.

"Stable your horse in back, and I'll show you the room," Drain said, and Fargo took the Ovaro into the stable, which he found roomy enough and neater than he'd expected. He unsaddled the horse, found a feed bag of oats for him and a pail of water, and when he returned to the inn he passed the two bodyguards who watched him with disdain in their eyes. Bert Drain waited inside the inn, a woman beside him, tall, olive-skinned, black eyes, and long black hair, handsome with even, strong features that fairly shouted Mexican and Indian blood. "This is my woman, Areta," the man said, and Fargo nodded to the woman. She returned a steady, appraising gaze that seemed to say she knew her strong, tall figure and breasts that pushed out her blouse was beyond ignoring. "She's just cleaned the room for you," Drain said, and Fargo suddenly caught the smell of whiskey from him. "She'll show you to it," he said and moved away as Fargo followed Areta down a short corridor. She walked with her back very straight, her rear hardly moving beneath the straight skirt, and opened the door of a room at the end of the corridor.

He saw a full-size bed, a porcelain pitcher of water, and a weathered bureau. A single window looked out one side of the inn. "You need food?" the woman asked, her voice low, almost hoarse.

"I could stand a sandwich," he said.

"I'll get it," she said. "Bert will charge extra."

"Fair enough," Fargo said.

"I'll bring it," she said.

"Just leave it. I'm going to have a look at the trading post, might even buy something," Fargo remarked.

She started to turn and paused. "He drives a hard bargain," she said, and Fargo nodded. "Do not try to fool him. He is a mean man."

"Thanks," Fargo said. "You always so helpful to strangers?"

"You do not look like most who pass this way," she said. "He does not believe you look for a mail route. He is smart. He has a feel about people."

"I thought you were his woman," Fargo said.

"I am, and I know him, enough to hate him," she said with sudden bitterness in her voice.

"Then why don't you leave him?" Fargo asked.

"Areta, goddammit, get out here," Bert Drain's shout interrupted. "Now, goddamn you, bitch."

"I have my reasons," she tossed to Fargo as she hurried from the room. He followed leisurely and saw Drain snarl at her as she reached him.

"Kenny and Carl want their damn supper," he said. Areta passed him without answering and disappeared into a kitchen. Drain turned as Fargo came up to him. The man composed his face, pulling the truculent anger from it. The whiskey odor was stronger, Fargo detected, then he saw the pint bottle protruding from the man's hip pocket.

"Knew a man who used to ride these mountains,

name of Josh Gibson," Fargo said casually. "I would imagine he stopped here."

"He might have. I don't recollect everybody who comes by," Drain said, and Fargo grunted silently. Drain didn't get so much traffic that he wouldn't remember those who came by, especially someone who regularly passed through. He strode from the inn and started for the trading post, and Drain hurried to catch up with him. "Got a mind to buy some things?" the man asked.

Fargo halted just inside the doorway of the small store, and his glance swept the clothes, gunbelts, boots, rifles, snowshoes, and Indian blankets that lay in casual array in the shop. "I don't see what I'd want," he commented, and Drain stepped forward, greed sliding across his face at once.

"And what'd that be?" the man questioned.

"A saddle. Looking for a real fancy saddle. Always wanted one, only they always cost too damn much," Fargo said.

"Well, now, I just might have what you want, mister," Bert Drain said and hurried into a small adjoining room. He returned carrying the saddle with him and dropped it on the floor in front of Fargo. "How's that?" he asked with avaricious triumph in his voice.

Fargo's eyes swept the carving in the back of the cantle, the hand-stitched skirt, and the silver horn. It was the saddle Jim Gibson had described to him, down to the fancy stitching along the edge of the cantle. He was about to close a hand around Drain's shirt when he heard the sound behind him and saw the two men enter, hands resting on their guns. "The woman said you'd come here," the one called Kenny grunted. "Any trouble?"

"No, no, the man wants to buy a fancy saddle," Drain said.

Deciding the two men had the position and the odds, Fargo set aside his first impulse. "Sure is what I'm looking for," he said to Drain.

"Fifty dollars," the man said, and Fargo let a low whistle sift through his pursed lips.

"That's pretty steep, friend," he muttered.

"It'd cost you twice that anywhere else," Drain said.

"How'd you come by it?" Fargo asked. "I don't want to be buying stolen saddles."

Fargo almost smiled at the expression of shock and hurt that Drain let cross his face. "Stolen? Not here. I don't sell any stolen goods. I bought it from a feller said he'd bought a fancier one."

Fargo cast a glance at the two men. They were still half behind him, watching suspiciously. Distrust was part of their job. It was also part of their nature, he decided. "Fifty dollars," he said. "Let me sleep on it, and we'll talk again come morning."

"Fine with me," Drain said, returned the saddle to the small storage room, and followed Fargo as he walked back to the inn. The two men tagged along a few paces behind and halted at the door of the inn.

"I'll be turning in," Fargo said. "Good night."

Drain nodded, and Fargo strolled down the short corridor to his room. He heard Drain talking to his two bodyguards as he closed the door of the room. The sandwich and a glass of water was atop the dresser. Good, sharp ham, he saw as he took the first bite. He finished the sandwich, washed it down with two long pulls on the water, and carefully opened the door of the room. The inn was dark except for a lamp that was burning in the entranceway, and Fargo crept down the hall, pausing every few feet to listen. He heard the sound of voices coming from a room just off a second corridor, and he crept along the wall until he reached the room. As he halted outside the door, the voices become more distinctive, Drain's guttural cursing first. "Goddamn, goddamn," the man swore. "Goddamn bitch. You wait. I'll do it."

"I laugh at you," he heard Areta say and then heard a sharp cry of pain at the sound of the blow. "Bastard," she flung out, and Fargo heard her half-leap and Drain's curse of anger, then the sound of a fall.

"Just had one drink too many, damn you," Drain shouted.

"One drink too many every time. Fool," Fargo heard Areta say, her voice ice, and then he heard Drain's roar of rage and the sound of his charging form slamming into the wall, then the woman's cry of pain. "Beat me, it's all you can do," she said as she gasped again in pain.

Fargo lifted one hand and knocked sharply on the door. The sounds from inside the room stopped, and then Drain's voice came. "Who the hell's there?" the man said.

"Fargo. Couldn't sleep thinking about that saddle," Fargo said.

"See me in the morning," Drain called.

"No. I won't sleep till I know it's mine. I've got the money here," Fargo said. The door opened a few seconds later. Drain wore only trousers, and inside the room the woman wore a white cotton nightdress torn along one side, but she still managed to look handsome and somehow dignified. Fargo pushed into the room and closed the door as Drain eyed him truculently.

"Let's have the money. Fifty dollars," the man muttered.

Fargo's hand shot out and struck Bert Drain in the chest, and the man slammed into the wall, surprise flooding his face. "Where the hell is Josh Gibson?" Fargo bit out.

"What the hell's wrong with you?" Drain said thickly.

"Josh Gibson. What's happened to him?" Fargo demanded.

"I don't know what the hell you're talking about," Drain said. "And nobody pushes me around." He swung, a short left hook that Fargo easily parried, sinking his own underhand right into the Drain's solar plexus. "Jesus," Drain wheezed as he went down on both knees.

"The saddle, how'd you get it?" Fargo asked.

Drain started to push to his feet, then dived forward, tackling Fargo around the knees, and the big man felt himself go backward. His head struck the wood side of the bed a glancing blow, enough to make him see colored lights for a moment, and then he felt Drain's hands around his neck. "Goddamn, I'll teach you to mess with me," Drain snarled. Fargo let himself go backward and half turned as his back landed on the floor. He got his shoulder into Drain's belly and pushed. The man's hands loosened, and Fargo brought one knee up, drove it into Drain's groin, and Drain fell away. He was mean and vicious, but without real strength, and Fargo let go a left shot that traveled in an arc to smash against the side of the man's head. Drain fell away, and Fargo was after him instantly, yanking him around by the shoulder to drive another short, hard blow into the man's abdomen.

"Oh, Christ," Drain gasped as he rolled, doubled up on his side with his hands clutching himself.

"What the hell happened to Josh Gibson? Answer me or I'll beat you to a pulp," Fargo said as he glanced up to see Areta watching from a corner of the room, her handsome face impassive.

"Don't know," Drain gasped out.

"You have the saddle. One more chance, Drain," Fargo threatened.

"Bought the saddle from Roy Coulter," the man breathed. "That's all I know."

Fargo reached down and yanked Bert Drain to his feet. "Where can I find Roy Coulter?" he asked.

"I don't know. Nobody knows where to find Roy Coulter," Drain said. "He's a wild man, lives up in the mountains."

"He tell you where he got the saddle?" Fargo questioned.

"No," Drain said.

"And you didn't ask."

"No."

"You knew he wouldn't have a fancy saddle like that," Fargo said.

"Folks want to sell, I buy," Drain said.

Fargo grunted. It was likely that the man was finally telling the truth. His kind seldom asked the origins of what they bought, and the army had corroborated the fact that Coulter was some kind of mountain Gypsy. "I find you've been lying to me, I'll be back," Fargo said, turned, and started for the door. He had almost reached it when he heard the sound behind him. He whirled and saw Drain rushing at him, a whiskey bottle in his upraised hand. Fargo had time only to twist his head to one side as Drain brought the bottle down in an arcing blow. It smashed against the door, the sound of it mingling with Drain's curse. Fargo brought an uppercut up that landed on the man's jaw, but not squarely in the close quarters. Yet Drain staggered back and Fargo smashed a chopping blow to the side of the man's head. Drain swayed and started to topple sideways when Fargo's lightning left landed flush on his jaw.

Drain arched backward as he fell, his head hitting hard against the edge of a chair. Fargo stood before his inert form on the floor and saw the vein throbbing in the man's temple. "He's alive, but it'll be a spell before he comes around," Fargo said as Areta came closer.

"I'll go to your room with you," she said, and Fargo fastened a glance of curiosity on her. "It will be an exchange," she said. "I can help you."

He shrugged, pulled the door open, and walked from the room. She came with him, and when he reached his room he slid the latch bolt closed and turned to face her. "You said you had your reasons for staying with him," Fargo remarked.

"Yes," the woman said. He watched her nightgown rise as she drew a deep breath. Her black eyes bored into him, and there was no shame in her handsome face. "I have a young sister in Texas. Good people are raising her, caring for her. I send them ten dollars a month, more if I can. Drain agreed to pay me that if I'd go with him. I have only a year left until my sister is old enough to go on her own."

"You could earn the money somewhere else," he said.

"Maybe. I was afraid to try. Sending her money every month was more important," the woman said.

Fargo nodded. She was as strong inside as she was

handsome outside. "You said we'd be exchanging," he reminded her.

A half-smile slid across her face. "I want you. I want to lay with you. The wanting came the minute I saw you," Areta said. "I can tell you where you might find out about Coulter, where he lives in the mountains. Exchanging." Fargo's eyes met hers, but he didn't answer, and her smile widened. "I know what you're thinking," she said.

"What's that?" he asked.

"You don't want to lay with anyone who's lain with the likes of Bert Drain," she said. He smiled, a hint of sheepishness in the smile at her accuracy. "You won't be," Areta said. "He has never been with me. He can't. I don't know why, but he can't. All he does is try and fail and drink and fail again. I think that's why he is so vicious a man. He makes up for his failings in cheating and beating and hurting others." She stepped forward, came to him, and her arms lifted, slid around his neck, and her lips pressed his mouth, and he instantly felt the trembling wanting of her. "It's been so long, so long," she breathed as her hands pulled at his shirt.

He let his gunbelt fall to the floor and undid the buttons of his jeans. It was wrong to turn away from a good deed, he murmured silently. Areta stepped back, pulled the nightgown from her, and he took in a handsome body, strong, well modeled, broad shoulders, and breasts that held a slow curve, filling out at the cups, with deep, purplish red nipples against her cream-olive skin, a flat abdomen, wide hips, a womanly figure. Where her strong thighs began an almost wild, dense mound seemed to spring outward, as if it tried to emulate the cascading of her long, jet black hair. He sank onto the bed with her, and his hand

46

cupped one firm breast, his mouth closing over one red-purple tip.

"Oh, oh, my God . . . yes, yes, oh, yes," she gasped, and her voice began a moaning sound as he pulled and caressed. Her hands were rushing up and down his body, pressing, touching, sliding, as if she were trying to draw in the feel of every part of him. Her hands came down over his muscled torso, down further, and closed on his pulsing warmth, and Areta gave a sharp cry of pure delight. She pulled on him, caressed, pulled again as she cried out and moaned, and her long, black hair flew from one side to the other as she tossed her head. "Jesus, God, oh, yes, oh, oh . . . ooooooh," Areta called out, and her body arched backward and half rose as she pulled at him, drew him over her, and called out again as he rested against the thick, dense black triangle. He felt her pubic mound, pressing upward, a throbbing hillock of desire, and he felt the thick, wild tuft close around him, and then she was sliding upward, bringing the olive-skinned thighs up around him, offering the warm, wet portal, and he responded. "Aaaaaah . . . aiiiii," Areta cried out as he slid forward, her hips lifting, thrusting upward at once, pumping with instant fury.

"Yes, yes, yes," she half screamed as she clutched him to her, firm thighs clasping him, arms pulling his face onto her purplish red nipples. She rose and fell under him, pumped with furious desire, screamed, and moaned, and the long black hair whipped against his face as she grew wilder and wilder. But it was not an inchoate wildness. In her lovemaking there was not just the wanting, but the strength inside her, a power to her passion, a sinew to her sex, and when she thrust her strong body upward, and her moans became a triumphant cry, she swept him along with her in the force of her climax.

When she fell back onto the bed, her thighs still holding him in their grip, her jet black hair fell half across her face, and the purplish red nipples quivered. She pulled his face down to her breasts, held him there as her body relaxed and her thighs finally fell open and away from his body. He slid down beside her, one hand moving along the smoothness of her olive skin, and she uttered a deep sigh of satisfaction as she rose up on one elbow and leaned herself against him. "It was everything, everything. I knew it would be that way with you. A woman knows those things," she said.

"Not all women," he smiled.

"All women," she insisted. "Some just refuse to admit what they know inside, not even to themselves."

"What about Drain? Will he take it out on you?" Fargo asked.

"No. He will be quiet for a while. Your beating will do that to him, and I will leave when the time comes. Nothing has changed," the woman said.

"Good," Fargo said as he again felt the quiet strength of her.

"And now my part of the exchanging," Areta said. "This man Coulter, he is a wild man, as wild as the mountains. He lives somewhere in Owl Mountain."

"Where's that?"

"It is the biggest mountain behind Lost Trail Pass. You will see it," she said.

"How do you know Roy Coulter lives there?" Fargo asked.

"Sometimes Shoshoni women come to trade Indian blankets for millet, usually before the winter comes. They talk Crow to trade, and I know a little Crow,"

Areta said, and Fargo nodded. Crow talk was the most common used in dealing with white men, and most tribes knew a little of it in addition to their own language. It was essentially a variation of Sioux. "Sometimes they talk of this man Coulter, but you will never find him. It is the woman you must find," Areta said.

"The woman?" Fargo frowned.

"Yes. She is the only one who will know where this man Coulter lives. It is said she knows everything about the mountains."

"Who is this woman?"

"No one knows, but she lives in the mountains, some say as wild as the animals. Some who have passed through have said they saw a flash of her. Trappers have caught sight of her, and the Shoshoni have often seen her."

"Does she have a name?" Fargo queried.

"She has many names. Some call her the woman of the mountains. Trappers call her the ghost girl. The Shoshoni call her *wakan tanka wohpe*, the spirit woman. They say she has special powers only the thunder god can give. They are afraid of her." Fargo smiled. Superstition, fear of the unknown, they were the ancient seeds from which legends sprang. He watched as Areta rose and pulled on the torn nightgown. "I will go back now. It has been good. Your stopping here has been good," she said. She smiled as he rose and pressed herself against him for a quick moment.

"I hope so," he said.

"Be careful in the morning," she said. "He is a small and vengeful man."

"He won't face me down. He hasn't that kind of courage," Fargo said. "But he has his two bodyguards. I know that. I'll be ready." She nodded and slipped from the room, and he put the latch bolt on again and stretched out on the bed, the smell of her still strong on the warm sheet. He'd have to be ready for trouble come morning. He knew that. Drain wouldn't just let him walk away. It wasn't a question of whether he'd strike back, just where. Fargo pulled sleep around himself. The day would dawn soon enough, he knew.

3

He washed and dressed as the morning sun found its way into the room, and he slid into the corridor with his hand on the butt of the Colt at his side. He scanned the short corridor amd moved carefully into the large room, sweeping the space with a lightninglike glance. Areta appeared at the door of the kitchen. "They wait for you to go to the stable," she whispered, and Fargo nodded. It was the one place he'd have to appear.

"Is there a back door to the stable?" he asked.

"No," she said.

"Is Drain with them?" Fargo asked, and she nodded.

"Can I get to the roof?" he queried.

"Yes," she said and pointed to a narrow flight of stairs that led upward along one wall of the building. "There is a door that opens onto the roof."

He blew her a kiss as he took the narrow stairway two steps at a time. It led to an attic, and another, shorter stairs brought him to a door that pushed upward and out onto the slanting roof. The shingles were weathered but still holding, and he crawled on his stomach to where the rear of the roof met the roof of the stable, some ten feet lower. "Damn," he swore softly. He had forgotten that the stable was attached to the inn. There was no place to climb down at the rear of the stable, which was what he had planned on doing. If he tried lowering himself down the sides, they would almost certainly see him and pick him off as though he were a fly on a wall. But he had to get into the stable without going around to the front where they waited. His eyes narrowed as he scanned the roof of the stable. It was badly in need of repair, the boards cracked, some splintered, many with their ends bending upward.

Swinging his long frame over the edge of the inn roof, he hung for a moment, then let himself drop to the stable, landing on the balls of his feet. He flattened himself instantly, crept forward a few feet to where he found a pair of boards that were barely attached. He pulled on the first one, and it came up easily. The second offered only a little more resistance. With both boards removed, he could see down into the stable where a crosswalk appeared beneath him, and below that a hayloft with no hay in it. Just below the hayloft he saw the mostly empty stable; the Ovaro was in the corner stall where he had put him.

Fargo moved carefully as he had to pull a third board loose to make an opening large enough for him to fit through. The third board creaked as he worked it loose, and he halted, listened, and resumed his task more cautiously. The board finally came loose, and he slid it aside, lowered himself through the opening, and dropped to the crosswalk. From there he climbed down to the hayloft and then down a short ladder to the stable floor. Moving quietly, he saddled the Ovaro, moved the horse out of the stall, and still on foot, he peered through the crack between the stable doors. His eyes swept the trees across from the stable, certain the two men were there waiting for him to come around the inn to approach the stable.

They probably planned to wait for him to reach the stable doors before opening fire. Perhaps Drain was also in the trees, ready to shoot from a different angle. Fargo's brow furrowed in thought. He had thought to race out on the Ovaro, but now he saw there was not enough distance to reach a full gallop without taking the bullets of what might be a cross fire. There were certainly two, maybe three, gunslingers waiting. He had to reduce the odds first. That took only patience. None of the three were hunters, not even trappers. They were cheap, vicious gunslingers who knew nothing about waiting, stalking, tenacity. They knew only about quick dry gulching, and he sank down on one knee, his eye glued to the crack between the doors.

His evaluation proved entirely accurate as, in but a few minutes, he saw the leaves move at the right as Bert Drain appeared. He headed for the inn, walking quickly, disappeared from sight for a few minutes, and then reappeared. He was running, this time toward the trees, beckoning with one arm. "He's not there. Goddamn, he must've gone around back," Fargo heard Drain call, and the trees parted a few feet to the left, and the two men emerged, both with guns in their hands. Drain barked orders, and Fargo saw the two men start to run in opposite directions to circle the inn from both sides. He raised the Colt, kicked the stable doors open, and fired.

The one called Kenny pitched forward in midstride, sprawling along the ground followed by a trail of red. The other one whirled, shock in his face, and started to empty his gun toward the stable doors. But he fired wildly, out of haste and fear. Fargo heard the bullets strike the wood of the doors as he aimed and fired. The man flew backward, perhaps three feet, before he went down onto his back. He kicked for a moment

53

and then lay still. Fargo turned, leaped onto the Ovaro, and sent the horse from the stable at a fast trot, the Colt in his hand. Bert Drain stared at the two figures on the ground, his face drained of color. He looked up at the big man on the Ovaro coming at him, and let the gun in his hand fall to the ground, terror in the grayness of his face. "No, Jesus, no," he breathed, and Fargo drew the horse to a stop.

"This is your lucky day. I'm going to let you live," Fargo said.

"It was their idea," the man weaseled.

"Don't lie. I might change my mind," Fargo said calmly, and Bert Drain swallowed hard and fell silent. "Do right by your woman. I'll be back," Fargo said and turned the Ovaro away as the man nodded, relief flooding his face. The veiled threat would suffice, for a while at least, Fargo knew. Drain was a fearful man. He'd stay that way for a while. He spurred the Ovaro on and soon climbed upward and left the town of Last Chance behind. He rode slowly through Lost Trail Pass as the land rose in steep steps and the richness of the land surrounded him, thick greenery everywhere, and he saw brown bear and antelope, large moose, and fleet-footed deer, mostly mule deer.

With all its lushness it was a forbidding land, somehow a fitting place to seek a will-o'-the-wisp woman, a female of rumor, old trappers' tales, and superstition. As he rode through the pass and the day wore on, he saw the character of the tree cover slowly change, bur oak, hackberry, dwarf maple, and serviceberry giving way to Engelmann spruce, quaking aspen, blue spruce, and Douglas fir. The mountain brush changed, also, growing more wiry, thicker, more inhospitable. Indian pony prints continued to cross the trails he rode, and as the day ended he emerged from the other end of the pass to face the tallest of three mountains that seemed to surround him.

"Owl Mountain," he murmured aloud. He felt the power and strength of the land sweep over him. He hurried upward along a trail and found a spot to bed down as the sun disappeared over the high peaks. He ate some of the beef jerky in his saddlebag and stretched out on his bedroll as the moon rose to turn the land into a place of pale silver and black shadows. He heard the howl of a timber wolf not far away, and he was beginning to drop off to sleep when the sudden, bloodcurdling scream of a cougar rent the air. His hand closed around the Colt at his side as the cry died away, and he took a long moment to let his muscles relax. He slept finally, until the sun crept over the mountain tops, and he woke to the chatter of redwings and Bullock's orioles.

He found a mountain stream of crystal clear freshness, and he washed, refilled his canteen, and finally rode up a trail where a pair of pronghorn antelopes leaped across his path. Owl Mountain became a place filled with trails, not all steep, but many dangerously narrow and dropping off with sheer sides. He had reached a place where the mountain leveled into a narrow level stretch. He put the pinto into a trot. At the far end of the small plateau when he reined up in surprise he saw a one-horse buckboard climbing up a trail below. A woman held the reins, a little girl of some seven or eight years old sitting beside her, traveling bags in the back of the rig.

She was in trouble. The trail was barely wide enough to keep the buckboard's wheels from skidding off the edge. But she had the sense to keep the horse moving slowly, and Fargo spurred the Ovaro over the edge of the plateau and down toward the woman. He slowed as he neared her and saw the tight strain in her rather plain face as she tried desperately to keep the horse pulling away from the edge of the trail. He had the Ovaro at a walk, and moved toward her as he debated what he could do to help. There wasn't a hell of a lot, he muttered silently. The narrowness of the trail gave him no room to come up alongside her. He had just decided to dismount and take the horse by the cheek strap to both calm and lead the animal when he saw the left front wheel of the buckboard roll over a stone, skid, and come down off the edge of the trail. The rear wheel followed at once as the woman pulled the horse to a halt.

Fargo swung from the pinto, halted some ten feet from the buckboard, and he spoke soothingly to the horse as he saw the animal feel danger, its eyes widening, its head stretching upwards, "Easy, now, easy . . ." Fargo murmured as he stepped to the horse. He slowly pressed the palm of his hand upon the animal's neck and let his touch communicate. The horse stopped stretching its neck upward as Fargo stroked soothingly. The woman still held the reins, but she sat frozen on the seat, the little girl clutching at her. Fargo glanced at the buckboard again and grimaced. The wagon tilted to the left as both wheels on that side were over the edge. Any movement on their part would send the wagon plunging.

The woman remained frozen in place on the seat with the little girl touching her, terror and pleading in her eyes as she stared at him. He wanted to make sure she stayed that way. "Don't move," he said.

"For how long?" she asked. "Maybe we can jump out the other side."

"You won't be able to make it. That buckboard

goes it'll take you, the girl, and the horse with it," he said.

"Maybe you can get him to pull the wheels up," she said.

"No," Fargo said, peering at the wheels over the edge. "He pulls, and the rear end of your rig will swing out and go over." He saw the helpless terror in her as she stared back, a plain-looking woman in her mid-forties, he guessed. "You stay where you are and let your weight hold your rig in place," he said as he reached down and drew the razor-sharp, double-edged throwing knife from its calf holster under his trouser leg. He edged forward beside the horse, keeping one hand against the animal's neck as he reached forward with the knife. "I'm going to cut the bellyband," he said, and saw that he could just manage to reach the strap that circled the horse's midsection. It was a thin, light bellyband, he noted gratefully as he began to cut into the leather, using the knife blade in short, sawing motions. "Easy now, easy," he murmured to the horse as the animal tossed its neck and head and then calmed again.

Fargo cut at the thinnest part of the leather, where the band circled the belly of the horse. Despite the sharpness of the knife, the cramped position made only short, back-and-forth movements possible, and his brow was beaded with perspiration when he saw the last edge of the leather strip parted. He watched as the bellyband fell to hang down from the horse's sides. "Don't move," he called to the woman. "I'm going to pull him forward now. The bellyband should just slide off him without pulling on the shafts." He took the horse's reins, flipped them over the animal's head, and gently began to urge the horse forward.

Fargo held his breath at the horse's first steps, his

eyes fastened on the wagon shafts. But they didn't move as the horse stepped out of the bellyband and the leather piece and the shafts dropped to the ground. He led the horse to where the Ovaro waited, draped the reins over the pinto's saddle horn, and returned to the buckboard. There was no longer the danger of the horse pulling at the buckboard. It was now a problem of weight and balance. If the woman rose with the little girl it would be enough to shift that precarious balance and send the rig plunging over the edge. Fargo's eyes narrowed as he studied the scene, and he finally stepped forward and carefully, almost gingerly, lowered himself on the front left corner of the buckboard floorboards. He felt his weight dip the wagon at once.

He spoke to the woman over his shoulder. "Send the girl first. Step down over the front, between the shafts. When she's down, you do the same. My weight ought to hold the wagon balanced enough to make up for yours. Move slowly," he said and pressed himself down harder as he felt the wagon shift ever so slightly when the little girl clambered down over the front. The woman followed, and he watched her swing down from the wagon and move up the path. Only when she cleared the shafts did he push to his feet, spin, and see the buckboard instantly slip sideways over the edge, free of the weight that had maintained its trembling balance.

He stepped to the edge and saw it smash into the bottom of the slope, cracking in two and the wheels spinning off in different directions. He turned to see the woman and the little girl beside him. "We'd be down there with it if it weren't for you," she said. "We're in your debt, mister. I'm May Korgan. This is my daughter, Eliza."

"Skye Fargo," he said. "What in tarnation were you doing in these mountains with a buckboard?"

"Came all the way across from the other side, from Spaulding. I followed the St. Joe for a little while. I got word my pa was real sick. Crossing the mountains was the only fast way to reach him."

"With a buckboard?" Fargo frowned.

"An old miner told me it could be done. It was dangerous, but I got this far," the woman said. "And now we've no buckboard and all our things are down there with it."

Fargo peered down the slope. It was steep, but there were plenty of stones and wiry mountain brush along the side. "I can get your things. We'll start with that," he said, and the woman clasped his arm.

"You know I can never repay you for all this," she said.

"Never worry about payment. It comes around, sooner or later, for the good and the bad," Fargo smiled and patted the little girl's head as she watched him with open, trusting eyes. "You two just stay here," he said as he lowered himself to the ground and slid his body over the edge of the slope. He felt with his feet and hands, found brush and rocks and began to descend, the steepness dictating caution, but the thick brush affording a good grip. He found a foothold for most of the way down, except for one section where he had to hang from brush clusters, and finally he reached the broken wagon at the bottom.

He slung the two traveling bags onto his back, grateful they both had long lengths of carrying straps, and began to pull his way upward. Halfway up he rested for a moment as he felt the strain on his shoulder and back muscles, and he glanced up to see the two faces peering apprehensively down at him. He drew a deep breath, clenched his grip around a wiry length of brush and continued the climb. May Korgan's hands reached down to help him when he came to the top, and she pulled on him as he lifted himself over the edge. He lay on his stomach for a moment, drawing in deep draughts of air, and then she took the traveling bags from his back as he sat up. "Thank you again," she murmured. "We have the horse. Eliza and I can ride him together."

"Let's get off this narrow damn trail, and then we'll talk," he said, pushing to his feet. He led the Ovaro up to the level land of the plateau while the little girl led their horse and May Korgan carried the bags. He found a place near the line of blue spruce that bordered one side of the plateau. He halted, and a quick glance showed him the sun nearing the top of the mountain. "I can't let you go on alone. You've just been plain lucky this far, and you saw how fast luck can run out," he said. May Korgan nodded glumly. "These mountains are Shoshoni hunting ground. You'd be fair game," he said. "I'll see you down to Lost Trail Pass. We'll meet an army patrol near there, I'm certain. Meanwhile, it'll be dark soon, and you two look like you can stand a rest. We'll bed down here."

"Yes, I'm trembling inside," the woman said.

"I'll come help you," the little girl said.

"If you like," Fargo nodded. She was a willing child, he saw, as plain-faced as her mother, but sweet and helpful. He paused to glance at May Korgan. He took the Colt from its holster and handed it to her. "While we're in the woods," he said. "Just in case."

"I don't know much about guns. I've never fired one," she said.

"An Indian shows, you just fire into the air," Fargo

told her, and she nodded as he disappeared into the woods. With Eliza helping, he gathered enough small firewood to last the night and carried it out with the little girl holding some. He stepped from the trees and halted, and the curse rose inside him. May Korgan sat on the grass, the Colt in her lap, her body stiffened, frozen in terror. Moving toward her, one stealthy, silent footstep at a time, was one of the largest and most beautiful cougars Fargo had ever seen.

The big cat, its lithe, tawny body stretched out, had its yellow eyes fastened on the woman, the tip of its tail twitching. It was well within easy pouncing distance of May Korgan and himself, and the woman was too paralyzed to fire even one shot into the air. Fargo felt helplessness surge through him as he let the wood slide from his arms. The yellow eyes flicked to him, and he cursed silently. Cougars were quick to turn away from danger, but once they had fixed on a prey they seldom turned aside. But he had nothing to lose by trying. He took a step forward. The big cat's lips drew back, and the growl sounded like the rumble of a volcano. Fargo halted, not daring to provoke an attack any more quickly than it would come of itself.

Even in the face of its deadliness it was impossible not to be awed by the animal's magnificence; its body was a symphony of sleekness, its wide, tawny head with a V-shaped spot of black fur between the short, tufted ears. The cougar's eyes stayed on him, burning malevolence, and Fargo tensed his muscles, certain it was only seconds before the big cat leaped. His frown came instantly as the cougar suddenly took a step backward, paused, ears moving back and forth, and then turned with consummate grace and stalked away to disappear into the trees. Fargo stared after it in disbelief, and then a motion in the spruce at his right caught at the corner of his eye. He turned to glimpse a flash of yellowness against the dark green, a form shadowed in the trees for a moment and then gone. Or had he been imagining? No, he answered himself. There had been something there.

But it was gone now, and so was the cougar, and he walked to May Korgan and retrieved the gun from her lap. "I . . . I'm sorry," she said. "I couldn't move, couldn't do anything."

"I've seen cougars have that effect before, on people and on other animals," Fargo said as the last of the dusk began to slip away. He made a small fire, and May Korgan brought some dried beef from her traveling bag, which they heated and ate. She had a blanket for herself and the girl and undressed with modesty, yet no girlish coyness, and he saw a square-shouldered woman with breasts beginning to hang low. He undressed and lay on his bedroll a few feet from her.

"Good night, Fargo. You're a special person. You even make cougars back off," she said.

"I don't know why that cat turned away. It sure wasn't anything I did," he said, and then fell silent wondering about the flash of yellow in the dark green of the spruce. Had it been the ghost girl, the Shoshoni's spirit woman? Had the cougar picked up her presence and decided to retreat? It would be in character for the big cat. The unexpected could usually make a cougar back off. Only one thought grew firm in his mind. After he got May Korgan and her little girl to safety, he'd return here. Chasing will-o'-the-wisps had to start someplace and this was as good a spot as any. He drew sleep around himself. He woke in the middle of the night as he heard a cougar's scream spiral through the air, not very far away, and finally managed to return to sleep.

When morning came he found a cluster of apple trees, a surprise among the spruces and firs, and they all enjoyed the firm and tasty flavor of the sheepnose that somehow had found a spot to root down. With the woman and the child riding the horse from the buckboard, their travel bags slung around the Ovaro's saddle horn, Fargo led the way downward. He veered away from Last Chance as he rode through the pass. He halted often, sometimes to scan the terrain after he spotted fresh pony tracks, but mostly to peer into the distance for signs of an army patrol. He finally glimpsed the small spiral of dust, higher in the pass than he'd expected, and he led the way to intercept the column of dust. He was waiting at a crossroad as the patrol rode up, Captain Osgood at the head of the troopers.

"Fargo," the captain said, his youthful face serious. "I was just thinking about you."

"And I was looking for you," Fargo smiled.

"You first," the captain said and tipped his hat to May Korgan. "Ma'am," he said with proper politeness.

"This is May Korgan and her daughter. Their buckboard met one narrow mountain trail too many. They need an escort to safety," Fargo said.

"Certainly, ma'am," the captain said to May Korgan.

"I'm most grateful," she answered, and Fargo saw the relief in her face.

"Your turn," he said to Osgood.

"Came across an old trapper name of Jake Seitz. He was torn up just the way the other families you saw were, but I think you were wrong about it not being the Shoshoni," the captain said.

"Why?"

"He had a tent not far from here. There were pony tracks all around it, his boots and belt had been taken along with some of his gear. He also had a full head of reddish hair he doesn't have anymore. They scalped him."

Fargo's lips pursed in surprise. "I'd like a look for myself," he said.

"Sure," the captain said and turned to his troopers. "Sergeant, take six men and bring the ladies to the post. The rest of you come with me."

"Thank you again, Fargo," the woman called out, and Fargo waved to her as he rode off beside the captain, the other six troopers following. Osgood led the way up a steep trail that topped off at a cleared area of relatively flat land, the gray canvas tent in the center of it. Fargo dismounted as he reined to a halt. He stepped to the silent figure sprawled on the ground. His glance took in the unshod hoofprints and the things from the tent that had been dragged outside and strewn about.

He dropped to one knee before the lifeless form of the trapper and examined the terrible tears and slashes that mutilated his body. He reached out with one hand, ran his fingers over the wounds and the remains of the man's bloodied scalp. He rose as Osgood came up beside him. "Same as the others," the captain said.

"And so's my answer," Fargo said.

The captain's brow lifted. "How can you say that now?" Osgood asked. "Hell, their pony prints are all over the place. They scalped him. They stole what they wanted."

"Oh, they were here, and they did all those things," Fargo admitted. "But he was already dead, killed by something else. They came along after, found him, took what they wanted, and scalped him. But they didn't kill him."

"How can you be so damn sure?" Osgood frowned.

"The blood of the wounds across his body is dried and cool. The blood around his scalp is still sticky and warm. I'd guess he was dead at least six hours before the Shoshoni came onto him, maybe more," Fargo said.

The captain stared at the trapper's lifeless form. "You still think it was a cougar?" he asked.

"Sure seems so," Fargo said. "You're right, there are plenty of them in these mountains."

"It's still not the way they act," the captain said.

"There's always the exception," Fargo said and climbed onto the Ovaro as the captain swung onto his mount.

"We'll send the chaplain and a burial detail tomorrow," Osgood said. "You going back into the mountains?"

"Right now," Fargo said.

"Keep your eyes open. The Shoshoni are out there as well as cougars," the captain said.

"I will, and thanks for seeing to the woman," Fargo said, and he received a crisp salute as he rode on. He climbed his way back through the pass, and it was dark when he neared the spot where he had camped the night before. He bedded down and lay back, his eyes scanning the deep darkness of the trees. Mountain forests always made him feel that they were the keepers of their own secrets, but now the certainty was stronger than ever. Would they be the secrets he needed to uncover, he wondered. Or the kind of secrets that brought death instead of answers? He closed his eyes and slept, anxious to hurry the morning.

4

The sun flooded the mountains as he breakfasted on a cluster of wild plums he had discovered. The deep forests were a tapestry of green, the blue spruce, the quaking aspen, the juniper, the Englemann spruce, and the firs each with their own shade and texture. He slowly edged the Ovaro into the trees where he had glimpsed the flash of yellow, and the coolness of the forest enveloped him at once. His eyes scanned the forest floor, but it was too thickly carpeted with springy spruce needles and leaf cover to carry hoofprints. He let the horse wander through the trees and let his glance sweep the low branches for signs of broken ends.

There were a few, but they could have been caused by deer or moose, he realized, and he halted, sat silently on the horse, and listened to the forest sounds. He heard only the scurrying of gray squirrels, the clicking of ox beetles, and the hum of a hundred different kinds of insects. The distinctive call of the rufous-sided towhee echoed through the evergreens, and he steered the Ovaro in a wide circle that brought him out into clear land, where he caught the flash of sun on water. He rode forward and found a small lake, irregularly oblong in shape, where the blue spruce and aspen grew almost to its shores. The sun had grown hot, and the clear blue water beckoned. He slid from the Ovaro, swept the surrounding trees with a long glance, saw that nothing moved, and he shed clothes at the edge of the small lake. He set his gunbelt atop the jeans he had neatly folded over his shirt, and he had only his underwear left on as he stepped to the water's edge.

He was about to pull off the last garment when he heard the sound, a low, throaty sound somewhere between a purr and a growl, and he turned to see the cougar crouched at the edge of the trees, only its head and powerful shoulders visible. It was the same cat he had seen the day before, the distinctive black V of fur between its ears. Fargo stayed frozen as he met the cougar's baleful eyes. He held it for a moment and then flicked his own gaze to where the gunbelt lay atop his clothes. He measured distances, aware that if he dived for the gun it would surely trigger the big cat into attacking. He was closer to his gun than the cougar was to him, but he knew the cougar could leap twice as fast as he could and five times as far. But the big cat hadn't moved from its place just past the trees, and Fargo began to slide his foot toward the gun.

That's when she stepped from the trees, a few yards to the right. He saw long hair the yellow of cornsilk, and a tall, slender shape. He hadn't time to take in more. She was walking directly toward him. "No, get back," he shouted. "Get back." But she kept coming toward him, and he flicked a glance at the cougar. It moved out of the trees altogether. "Get out of here," he shouted at her, and she halted, her eyes going to the big cat.

Fargo heard the Ovaro snort and glimpsed the horse running to the end of the lake at the cougar's presence. Fargo eyed his gun again and cursed. The cougar had slunk closer, and then as he watched with surprise, the big cat rose up, straightened its long body out of its stalking stance. He strode toward the young woman, and Fargo felt himself swallow hard as the cougar rubbed itself against her thigh. "Yes, yes," he heard the girl say as she stroked the big cat's head with one hand.

"I'll be dammed," Fargo muttered as he felt the perspiration coating his torso, and he drew in a long breath. The young woman came toward him, the cougar at her side. He had time to take her in now, and he saw a young girl's face that was somehow also very womanly, a straight, short nose, pale lips, and light blue eyes that studied him as she came closer. It was an almost beautiful face, he decided, delicate, and with the cornsilk yellow hair, it had a pastel quality to it. But there was also a purity in it that seemed to come from some inner glow. She glided more than walked, and she wore a light beige dress of cotton that managed to cling even as it fell in a straight line around a very slender, tall body. High, small breasts made only a tiny protruberance under the round neckline of the dress.

She halted, and Fargo glanced at the cougar beside her and then back to the light blue eyes. No phantom, no folk legend. She existed, a very real and unusually lovely apparition. "Where is the woman and the child?" she asked.

"Gone their way," Fargo said. "Then it was you in the trees yesterday."

She nodded. "Why have you come back?" she asked.

"To find you," Fargo said.

Her lips formed a half-smile that was strangely shy yet sensual. "Because you have heard stories?"

"Yes, and because I've things to ask you," he said. He stood still as she moved and slowly circled him. Finally she halted in front of him again.

"You have beauty and power," she said, her words delivered not so much as a compliment but as a simple statement. "I admire beauty and power when they are one," she said and let her hand move along the cougar's back to emphasize her remark. "What have you heard about me?" she asked.

"Some say you are a ghost. The Shoshoni say you are *wakan tanka wohpe,* the spirit woman," Fargo answered.

The strange little half-smile touched her lips again. "What do you think?" she asked.

"I think you are very beautiful," he said.

"I am no ghost," she said.

"Definitely not."

"But I could be a spirit woman," she said, and he realized she was toying with him, quietly laughing.

"You could be," he said solemnly as he decided to go along with her.

"You were going to bathe in the lake. I interrupted you. Please go on," she said. "I want to watch."

Fargo shrugged. He wanted her cooperation. He'd indulge her, he decided, and he turned, stripped off his underwear, and dived into the lake. He went underwater and came up to see her standing, watching, the cougar now stretched out at her feet. He dived again, did a cartwheel in the water and swam closer to the shore. He felt the bottom under him and stood up in the water just below his waist. "This is my favorite lake. I think I'll join you," she said.

"Why not?" he said, trying to keep the surprise from his face. She stepped to the water's edge, lifted both arms, and pulled the dress up and over her head.

She wore nothing under it, and Fargo drank in her slender loveliness, long waist, long thighs, narrow hips, her skin a pale white, a small V under her flat belly, hardly more than fuzz, and her small breasts high and piquant, each tipped with an almost flat nipple of the palest pink on a tiny areola of matching paleness. She seemed a wood nymph, a water sprite, all glowing delicacy with her long cornsilk hair, and yet also possessing a shimmering sensuousness. She was a beautiful and strange physical admixture, a child woman, and he wondered if she were as totally unselfconscious as she seemed. "You often do this with someone you've just met?" he asked her.

"This is the first time," she said as she lowered herself into the lake, the small, high breasts just resting on the surface of the water, her light blue eyes meeting his gaze with open directness. "I have never come out to meet anyone," she said.

"Why have you done it now?" Fargo asked.

A tiny furrow touched her smooth brow. "I don't know. I must think about that," she said.

"I'm flattered," he said. "Aren't you afraid of what I might do?"

The little smile came again. "All I have to do is cry out," she said, and her glance went to the cougar for a second. He allowed wry appreciation to color his nod and watched as she sank under the surface, swam underwater, and came up a half-dozen yards away. He watched as she turned, dipped, and rose with smooth movements of sinuous grace, and he glimpsed flashes of long thighs, the small, firm rear, the petite breasts as she cavorted in the water, graceful as an otter. When she finally halted and began to swim toward shore, he stroked his way to where the Ovaro waited, pulled a towel from his saddlebag, and a smaller sheet for himself. He returned to where she had stepped onto the shore, the sheet tied around his groin, and handed the towel to her.

"Thank you," she said as she pulled the towel over herself and rubbed herself dry under it. He used the sheet, and when he turned back to her he had slipped into underdrawers and jeans. He saw her draw the simple sheath dress over herself.

"You satisfy a man's love of beauty, but you put a strain on his selfdiscipline," Fargo commented.

She frowned for a moment in thought. "I don't mean to do either," she said with the childlike directness again. She combined a special kind of naïveté with a special kind of wisdom, he decided.

"I can't go around calling you 'spirit woman'," he said.

"Dawn," she smiled. "That is my name. Dawn."

How very fitting, he thought silently. "Just Dawn?"

"Dawn Semple," she said.

"Where do you live, Dawn?" he asked.

"I will show you," she said, and her little smile was tinged with wonder. "I have never done that for anyone, either," she added. "Get your horse and come with me."

"I'll have trouble getting him near your cougar," Fargo said.

"Yes, I'm sure," she said. "My horse has learned not to be afraid, but it took me a long time."

"You go. I'll follow your trail," Fargo said.

Her smile was chiding. "No one has ever followed my trail," she said.

"Try me," he said.

She shrugged. "I'll come find you when you're lost," she said, and he watched her walk into the spruce, her slender form willowy beautiful, the cougar at her side. Fargo returned to the Ovaro, swung onto the horse, and slowly rode into the spruce where she had gone. He smiled at once. She knew how to tread against the tree trunks so not to leave footprints, a trick no white man except himself knew, and only a few Indians knew. But he spotted the soft slight scraping marks, and he also saw the still fresh paw prints of the cougar that made its way alone.

He rode slowly, taking pains to peer carefully at each tree, and saw where she turned and moved into deeper woods. She had grown a little overconfident now, he saw, leaving footprints from time to time as she climbed a slope. The blue spruce and aspen stayed thick, but he saw the slope level off, and then, through the trees, the house came into his view. Sturdy, stone and log, it set back on a small cleared circle, and he saw her kneeling down, handfeeding a pair of red foxes, and he shook his head in amazement. The foxes suddenly stopped taking food, turned, and darted away, and she rose. Her eyes were peering into the forest as he rode into the clearing. He enjoyed the surprise that filled the light blue orbs as she saw him.

"There's a first time for everything," he said.

"I'm without words," she said. "You must be very special."

"It's what I do best. Some call me the Trailsman," he said.

"I see why," she nodded, and he moved the Ovaro forward a few yards further before he swung to the ground.

"Where's your big cat?" he asked.

"Gone his way. He does not stay here. He comes and goes as he pleases," she said. Fargo's eyes went to the house again, and he saw the planted rows of vegetables that stretched out behind it. "Tomatoes, winter squash, camas root, potatoes, cabbage, lettuce, beans," she said. "I also grow onion, basil, and rosemary."

Fargo's eyes went to the house again. "You didn't build this," he said.

"No, I didn't. My father, with my mother's help," Dawn said.

"What happened? Why are you alone in these mountains?" he asked.

"My father came here to study and paint the birds. After the house was finished, he took sick. I don't know what it was. My mother fell ill soon after. They died almost together," Dawn said. "Some men came by when they were sick. I asked them to take me to find a doctor. Instead, they robbed us and took my father's boots and guns. Two other men passed, trappers. They wouldn't come near the house or me when I told them my folks were both sick. They just ran away."

"And you stayed on here," Fargo said.

"Yes. I wanted nothing more to do with humans. I wanted to stay here where it was beautiful, where we had come to be happy. I've always believed things happen for a reason. Most times we don't know that reason, but it's there. I felt things had happened for me to stay here, that this was the place for me. I was fourteen then. That was five years ago."

"You've never wanted to leave? Never wanted to rejoin the world?"

"I've watched men come through the mountains. They have made me happy I am here. I've seen them steal from each other, fight over gold, kill over possessions. I don't want that kind of world. This is my world," she said.

"There is killing here. This world is full of killing,

the strong kill the weak, one animal kills another to eat," he told her. "There is cruelty and viciousness here."

"Yes, but that is different. That is nature's way. There is no killing for greed, no cruelty for pleasure. Only need and survival rule this world, not hate, jealousy, power, greed," she answered, and he didn't pursue the exchange further as she glanced up at the sun. "I must be somewhere," she said. "Follow me, if you like, but stay back some."

He waited as she went into the house and returned carrying a half-dozen pieces of meat he recognized as wild turkey. She hurried off behind the house into the forest, and he stayed back a dozen yards as he followed up a steep path. She moved quickly, her steps agile, and he watched as the trees parted and she stepped into a clear place and onto a flat rock. The land dropped away beyond the rock, and from the spot one could see the high reaches of Owl Mountain and the terrain below. Dawn Semple spread her arms upward, a piece of the wild turkey meat in each hand, and she stood motionless, cornsilk hair flowing, as if she were a carving that grew out of the rock.

He caught the shadow of giant wings first, and then saw the soaring form drop down into sight, circle with a long, soaring glide, and come onto the rock to land at Dawn Semple's feet. Fargo stared at the magnificent beauty of the golden eagle, seeing it more closely than he ever had before. He studied its fierce eyes, the yellow- and blue-tipped beak, and the gold-flecked head feathers that became a dark brown over the rest of its body and wings. Dawn lowered her arms, and the eagle took the meat from her and instantly soared away in its powerful, soaring flight. The bird made two more trips to her, and when the meat was gone it returned once more. With talons that could rip a man's chest open, it lighted for a brief moment on Dawn's shoulder with a delicate touch and then flew away.

The scene could have been witnessed by anyone above on the mountain or in the terrain below, and he was certain the Shoshoni had seen it before. It was plain they had seen her way with the canny and wildly fierce creatures. It was little wonder they feared her and called her the spirit woman. Fargo found a sense of awe pulling at him as he watched. She evoked a bond with the wild creatures, reached out to them, responded to them, and they to her in some unexplainable way. A complete lack of fear? He frowned. A complete trust? An inner purity? Or some other arcane gift given her in ways beyond understanding? It didn't much matter. It worked and was part of the existence she had chosen for herself.

Chosen was not the right word, he realized. Thrust upon her was perhaps better, thrust by events, fear, resentment. It seemed a waste, nonetheless, that such loveliness should remain unseen and unappreciated. He knew what she'd answer to that. The wild columbine, the iris, and the cardinal flower bloomed with their loveliness whether seen or unseen. He waited as she came from the rock. She fell in step beside him as they returned to the house. He kept seeing her in his mind as she'd been at the lake, all delicate beauty glowing with an inner fire that was at once pure yet sensuous. Maybe purity and sensuousness were not contradictions, he frowned inwardly. It was something he'd have to think about more at another time. He had more immediate concerns now, and as if she had picked up his thoughts with an inner acuteness, she voiced the question as they reached the house.

"You said you had come back to ask me things," she remarked. "Come inside." He dismounted and followed her into a fair-sized room hung with wall hangings of handwoven cloth. A leather sofa was at one side and a bearskin rug in front of it. He saw two smaller rooms leading from the main room, on both sides of a large fireplace. "My mother liked to weave," she said, gesturing to the wall hangings.

Fargo nodded to a rifle in one corner and then to the bearskin rug. "Even you kill and hunt," he remarked.

"Only as all other creatures hunt, to live, to survive," she said, no defiance, but a firm belief that the laws she abided by were the proper ones and very different from man's. Maybe she was right, he conceded silently.

"Where did you get the rifle?" he asked.

"I took it from three men who killed each other in a gunfight on the other side of the mountain. I have another," she said.

"You'll run out of ammunition one day," he told her.

She shrugged. "I know, but I have learned to make sinew-backed bows," she said. "You did not come back to ask those things."

"No," he said and sat on a leather hassock as she folded herself gracefully atop the sofa. "I look for two men. One is called Josh Gibson. He passed through these mountains every month until he suddenly disappeared. I've reason to believe a man named Roy Coulter might have killed him. I'm told this Roy Coulter is a wild man who lives in these mountains and only you might know where." He paused and saw caution slide across her lovely features. "Do you know this Roy Coulter?" he asked.

"I have seen him," she said. "He would not kill anyone."

"How do you know that?" Fargo questioned.

"I know it," she said with simple firmness. "He is, as you have heard, a wild man. But he is not the kind to kill."

"You can't be sure of that," Fargo said.

"I know," she insisted.

"Can cougars kill people?" he asked.

"If they are attacked by people," she answered.

"Could they attack people just to kill?" He persisted.

"It is not their way," she said.

"Not the way of the grizzly bear, either," he said, and she nodded. "Yet grizzly bears have attacked people, killed for the pleasure of killing. They become what they call rogue bears . . . outlaws. It can happen with a cougar, too."

"No," she said.

"It happens to men all the time. You know that," he pressed, and she shrugged.

"To men," she conceded.

"Roy Coulter is a man," he tossed at her. "He could have turned outlaw. He could have killed." He saw the tiny lines pull at her mouth as she resisted the thought. "Cougars can kill. One has been killing people, entire families," he said and told her of the bodies he'd examined at the three cabins.

"Not my cougar, not Prince," she said instantly.

"Is that what you call him?" Fargo asked, and she nodded. "I didn't say it was him. I said you can't be sure. A cougar can kill, turn outlaw. You can't be sure, not about Roy Coulter, either," he said.

"No, none of them," she murmured as she frowned into space, her light blue eyes troubled. Her resistance was more than defensiveness, more than an unwilling-

77

ness to believe. It was not simply naïveté, either. It had its roots in what she was, that girl-woman, that mixture of innocence and purity that had let her make herself one with the mountain and its creatures. He'd seen the evidence with his own eyes. She had bonded with the creatures of wildness. They were her friends and she was theirs and that bonding embraced even strange wild Roy Coulter.

But innocence and purity were their own kind of blindness, he realized. He had to find a way to reach through that to her. But he had to be careful. For some reason, she had made contact with him. It was vital he keep that. It would be easy for her to vanish on him, and he didn't want that happening. He reached out, rested his hand on her arm, and she turned her troubled eyes on him, a moment's surprise in their light blue depths. "You're not being disloyal," he said gently. "It is just something you must recognize."

She rose, and he stood up with her, her face set, a frown on her smooth forehead. With one hand, she pushed back the long cornsilk hair. "I must think more about this," she said.

"Just tell me where I can find Roy Coulter," he pressed.

"No, not until I have thought more about what you have said and about everything else," she answered.

"Everything else?" he echoed with a frown.

"Yes. There are things I do not understand. I must think more about everything," Dawn said, and her voice was quietly firm. He'd do best not to press her, he realized, and he went with her as she rose and walked from the house.

"I'll come back tomorrow," he said, and she nodded, her sweet, lovely face wreathed in seriousness. She watched him climb onto the Ovaro, and she stood very still and very straight, her small breasts pressing tiny points into the dress. With her long yellow hair flowing in a soft wind that had come up, she somehow managed to look pure and innocent yet regal. Her eyes, unsmiling and troubled, followed him as he walked the Ovaro from the cleared space, and he left her with reluctance, yet knowing it was the thing to do.

He rode downhill, made his way through the thick blue spruce, found a trail that wandered downward, but in the open, and which let him survey the terrain. The day began to move into late afternoon, the sun leaving deeper shadows on the green tapestry of the mountain forests. He had ridden steadily downward for another hour when he spotted the slender thread of smoke rising straight upward from behind a tree-covered ridge. His eyes narrowed on the plume, too steady in its narrowness to be open campfire. It had to be from a chimney, he was certain, and he sent the pinto down to the ridge. When he pushed through the spruce and juniper, he spied the cabin in a small cleared area at the foot of the ridge. Sturdy saddle-notched logs met his gaze as he rode closer, and he saw two corrals behind the cabin, goats and hogs roaming freely in both.

A man came from behind the house as Fargo rode into the cleared space. He was young, bearded, and he was carrying a shovel. A woman with a baby in her arms stepped from the cabin door. "Howdy," he said. "Get yourself lost? It's easy to do up here."

"No. Saw your smoke. Name's Fargo . . . Skye Fargo."

"Ben Dryson."

"Has the army had a patrol up to visit you in the last week?" Fargo asked.

"No, they don't come up this far," Ben Dryson said.

"I met with Captain Osgood a few days back. There's been trouble. Three families have been killed," Fargo said.

"Oh, my God," the woman interrupted. "Down below?" Fargo nodded, and she gave a little gasp. "That'd be the Ferrises, for one," she said.

"The Shoshoni?" Ben Dryson asked.

"No. A cougar attack, I'm pretty damn sure," Fargo said.

"Cougar attack? Never heard of that before," the man said.

"One that's gone rogue and found man easy prey or lost its usual fear of humans," Fargo said. "I'd like knowing myself. If you've no mind I'd like to bed down near for the night. That way maybe we could do some surprising of our own."

"Well, we'd be beholden to you, Fargo. But you've got to break bread with us," the man said as his wife nodded.

"That'd be welcome," Fargo said as he dismounted. The sun slipped over the high peaks, and he went inside the cabin with Ben Dryson. The meal was solid and tasty, and they talked about the hardships and the rewards of carving a home out of the wilderness. The time came quickly enough when he went into the dark night and faded into the trees. He laid out his bedroll and stretched across it after taking the big Sharps from its saddle holster. With the rifle beside him, he lay on his stomach and faced the cabin so that as he catnapped through the long night, if something woke him he was ready to fire without a second's delay.

But nothing came during the night except the dark

and the silence. He catnapped, woke, watched, and listened and catnapped again, and finally the pink streaks of the new day touched the sky.

He rose, stretched, and returned the rifle to its case as Ben Dryson emerged from the cabin with the new sun touching the land. The night had been a disappointment and a blessing, an attempt to avoid sudden death and as such was no waste at all. He walked from the trees, and Ben Dryson greeted him alongside the stone well a dozen feet from the cabin. The man stripped to his underdrawers and washed with a bucket of well water. As he dried himself with a towel he called to Fargo, "You're next, friend. Sally will be inside with the baby for another few minutes."

Fargo stepped to the well, took off his gunbelt, and then his clothes down to his underdrawers. He used the water lavishly to wash, and, trousers on, Ben Dryson tossed him the towel to dry. "I'll get us some goat's milk," he said, hurrying around a corner of the cabin. Fargo had the towel over his head and was drying his hair and face when he heard the sound. It was just the faintest swish of air, and he knew what it was in an instant flash as his blood turned to ice. He threw himself down and forward, the towel still around his head. He felt the sweep of claws tear the towel away, and he glimpsed the tawny form sweep over him.

"Damn," he cursed as he hit the ground. "Goddamn," He rolled, the gun still more than an arm's length away under his clothes. He whirled on his back as he heard the cry of pain and saw Ben Dryson go down under the cougar's leaping form. "No, goddamn you, no," he shouted as he jumped to his feet and screamed again at the big cat. It was an inadvertent reaction that made him start to rush at it, but he skidded to a halt as, distracted by his shouting, the cougar whirled. It started toward him, and he gasped as he saw the dark V of fur between its ears. He dived sideways as the cougar charged, covering the ground with flying strides, and he flung himself onto the clothes and found the Colt, yanked it from the holster and fired from his back, wild, hasty shots, anything to make the cat swerve.

His bullets went wild as he emptied the Colt and he saw the cougar twist. But suddenly the big cat changed direction, landing with all four feet and turning again. Fargo managed to leap up, and he seized hold of the water bucket as the cougar charged him again. He stayed, his breath frozen inside him as the cat charged directly at him. It was but a stride away, huge fangs bared, hate in its yellow eyes, when Fargo flung the bucket with all his strength. It smashed into the cougar's face with just enough force to make the cat break its charge, giving Fargo precious split seconds to fling himself sideways. It also gave Ben Dryson's wife a chance to run out and fire a heavy plains rifle at the cat. Her shots missed, and with a last backward glance the cougar vanished into the trees.

Fargo lay on his side, letting his breath return as the woman rushed to where her husband had struggled to a sitting position, blood running down his shoulder. "Goddamn," Fargo swore aloud, at himself more than anything else. He had miscalculated. He had misjudged when he should have known better. It was all so plain now. "Dammit, dammit," he swore aloud again. It had always been there. He simply hadn't taken enough time to see it. None of the other families had been slain at night. They hadn't come from their beds partially dressed to investigate a noise. Nor had they been attacked while they slept. They had all been clothed and outside. He simply hadn't been seeing with his usual acute powers of observation. Perhaps he'd been too occupied with the nature of their wounds, too intent on showing they were not made by the Shoshoni.

The cougar was not normally a nocturnal hunter. It struck more by day than by night. He knew that, but again, the fact hadn't registered at the time. He hadn't seen clearly or thought right, and it had damn near cost him his life—and the Drysons' lives, too, though it was plain that they had been the big cat's next target. He'd have come for them sooner or later, and perhaps it was best he'd struck now. Fargo pushed himself to his feet and strode to where the woman was helping her husband into the house. Dryson was still bleeding heavily, and that was good, Fargo knew. It helped cleanse the wounds. He helped carry the man into the house and lowered him onto a bed.

"They're not too deep," Dryson said. "Damn cat was about to tear my throat out with its teeth when you got it to turn and come at you."

"We were all lucky in one way or another," Fargo said as the woman came in with warm water and cloths to clean the wounds further. Fargo stepped outside, dressed slowly and reloaded the Colt before stepping into the cabin again. Ben Dryson was sitting up, his shoulder and arm swathed in cloth bandages.

"Put birch compresses on it," the woman said. "He'll come back, won't he? He'll try again."

"No. I'll see to that," Fargo said, drawing their frowns. "I know that cat. I've seen it before. I know where it has a den." It was enough, he knew. He'd only sound as though he were a fool if he tried explaining all of it.

"We'd sure be grateful to you forever," Ben Dryson said.

"I'm just not sure how quickly I can track him down. You stay alert when you're outside the house for the next few days," Fargo said.

"You can be sure of that," Dryson said as he winced in pain.

"I'll stop back if I can," Fargo said as he started to the door.

"Good luck," the man called after him. He went into the trees, found the Ovaro not far away, and pulled himself into the saddle. It had not been a passing cougar. It had been a very particular cougar, and as he climbed the steep mountain trails he felt the grimness of his task settle over him. It would hurt her terribly when he told her that her cougar was a renegade, a rogue killer that had left the normal ways of the big cats. Would she believe him? The question hung inside him, no idle thought, but a very real possibility.

He frowned as the thoughts tumbled over one another. Where would her loyalties lie? She was more in spirit with the wild creatures than with humans. Would it be possible for her to believe him? He swore inwardly and wondered if he should stay silent about the cougar until she told him what he wanted to know about Roy Coulter. But what if she wanted more time to think, to wrestle with her inner uncertainties? He couldn't risk that. He couldn't play with the Drysons' lives that way. The cougar had struck at them. It would return to strike again. It had fixed on its prey, and its prey was still there. It would return. That was the way of the hunter.

He climbed the steep trail and Dawn Semple's house came into sight. The questions were still whirling inside him unanswered. "Damn," he swore with a grim helplessness.

5

He left the horse just inside the edge of the trees and stepped into the open where Dawn was hand-feeding a trio of white-tailed deer. The three deer looked up as soon as he appeared; then they backed away and bounded into the forest. Dawn turned to him, and he was encouraged by the small, almost shy smile she offered. She wore a dark red dress, not as straight as the other; it clung to her figure so that even the high, firm little mounds were outlined. Between the dress and her long cornsilk hair, she might have been a tall and lovely gladiola.

Fargo's hand rested on the butt of the Colt as he walked toward her. "Where's your cougar?" he asked, keeping his tone casual.

"He's not here. He doesn't come every morning. He has a den higher up on the mountain," she said.

He dropped his hand from the butt of the Colt and felt the moment of relief flood through him. "Done your thinking?" he asked.

"Only some," Dawn said.

"Enough to tell me where to find Roy Coulter?" he questioned.

"Roy Coulter did not kill the other man," she said.

"Josh Gibson," Fargo said.

"Whatever his name. I'm sure of it," she said.

"That's not enough. I have to be sure myself. A young woman's life depends on what I can find out," Fargo said.

"Roy Coulter is a wild child in the body of a man," she said.

"He sold the saddle from Josh Gibson's horse. How did he get it?" Fargo pressed.

The blue eyes blinked at him for a moment. "He found the horse. He is not a killer," she said. Fargo swore inwardly. She was being adamant, too certain to even entertain the possibility. He'd never get through to her unless he could shock her into doubting herself. He drew a deep breath and decided to take the plunge.

"You don't know that. You don't even know about that cougar of yours," he said.

"What do you mean?" she frowned instantly.

"He is a killer, and you don't know it," Fargo tossed at her.

"That's nonsense. You can leave if you're going to say things like that," she flared, and he grimaced inwardly. There was no turning back now.

"He's torn apart three families. He almost had a fourth last night," Fargo said.

"No. Maybe some other cougar, and I don't even believe that," Dawn frowned.

"I was there. I saw him, the dark mark between his ears. He tried to kill me," Fargo said and saw her recoil as if she'd been physically struck. Her round, light blue eyes speared him with disdain.

"Why are you saying these things? To trick me into telling where to find Roy Coulter? It won't work," she said coldly.

"I'm saying them because they're true," Fargo returned.

The round blue eyes stayed icy. "No," she said. "No."

"I can prove it if you give me the chance," Fargo said.

"How?" she asked warily.

"I tell you he tried to kill me just after dawn this morning. If I'm right, you know what will happen when he sees me again."

"He'll attack, of course. It will be the natural thing for him, for any cougar."

"Take me to that den. You'll see for yourself. It's the only way to prove it," Fargo said, and she frowned back.

"It'll prove you are wrong," she said.

"Then let's find out. I'll apologize if I am," Fargo said.

"All right. Follow behind me. Stay behind till I find him," she said.

"I'll get my rifle," he said.

"No," she snapped.

"I don't hanker to be killed to prove I'm right," he tossed back.

"The gun could make him attack. Animals know a weapon when they see one. They know it with their own wisdom," she said, and he nodded grimly as he conceded the point. They did know, and not just from experience. It was an intuitive thing that even a stick could trigger. "Besides, he will attack to defend me. He could think you are going to hurt me," she added.

"No rifle," Fargo growled and watched as she turned, the movement graceful as a fawn's. She walked past the house and into the forested slope behind it, and he waited, then followed in her tracks. He stayed back far enough to glimpse her as she made her way up the slope and turned, following a narrow deer trail for a while, and then climbing again through large Englemann spruce. The slope grew less steep and almost leveled off, and he saw her slow and move onto a stone ledge; behind it was the mouth of a large cave. He moved forward carefully, silently, and dropped to one knee as he saw Dawn halt and wait until the big cat sauntered from the cave.

It came to her as she extended one arm, rubbed itself against her leg as she stroked its ears and ran one hand across its head. Fargo saw the dark V of fur again. No mistake, he muttered silently, no other cougar. He crept forward a few paces closer and halted again as the cougar suddenly stopped rubbing against her. It backed away, its eyes searching the surrounding trees with the baleful yellow glow. It went into a stalking motion, body lowered, ears flattened, the end of the long tail twitching its black tuft. "There, now, all right, all right," Fargo heard Dawn say, her voice low and soothing. She moved to the cougar and started to run her hand down its neck. The cat stepped away and hissed. "Prince," Dawn said, a note of firmness coming into her voice. "Easy, handsome one . . . easy. It's all right."

The big cat stayed in place this time as she came to it again, her hand soothingly pressed along the tawny back, but Fargo heard the low growl that rumbled from deep inside it. "Shhhh . . . shhh, it's all right," Dawn said soothingly. Fargo drew the Colt, held it in his hand, his arm extended downward, as he rose and walked out onto the ledge of rock. He saw the big cat turn and dart away toward its den. Then it whirled and faced him, lips drawn back. Fargo's glance went to Dawn. She stared at the cougar, and he saw the surprise in her face. "All right, it's all right," she said and stepped toward the big cat. But the cougar's growl rose, and it flattened lower, and Fargo saw the powerful shoulder muscles ripple. It was going to charge.

"Look out," he yelled at Dawn as he brought the Colt up.

She threw a glance back at him as she stood between him and the cougar. "Don't shoot," she said. She turned back to the big cat and spoke sharply to it this time. But Fargo saw the tawny blur as the cougar charged. Dammit, she was between him and the cat, blocking a clear shot. But the cat swerved past her as it came in great leaping bounds, and Fargo fired, two shots to see if they'd be enough to turn it away. They were as the cougar whirled, spun around, and then around again. But it was charging again, Fargo saw, and Dawn's slender shape was racing to intercept the big cat. "No, down, down . . . you hear me, down," she was shouting. But the cougar neither listened nor did he swerve as she came before him. Teeth bared, he sprang at her, and Fargo fired from one knee to steady his arm.

He'd had only split seconds to aim, but he saw his first shot slam into the cougar's neck just below its head. The animal half turned in midair as Dawn fell backward to the ground. Fargo's second shot hit the cougar in the side of its head. His next shot pierced the big cat in almost the exact same spot. He had only one bullet left in the chamber, but he saw the cougar twitch, its great body shudder and lay still. Dawn pushed to her knees, not more than a few feet from the silent form. She went to it, leaned across the great tawny form, and her hands stroked the muscled beauty of it as her muffled sobs drifted to where Fargo waited.

He rose and reloaded the Colt, and waited until she rose before he walked to her. The tear stains were on her face, but she met his eyes with her open directness. "You were right," she said softly.

"He would have killed you," Fargo said. "You were in his way."

"I do not understand. I do not know what to think," she said.

"It has hurt, I know," Fargo said gently.

"I must have time alone," she said.

"It may not be a time to be alone," he offered.

"Come to see my tonight. I must think alone," she said, and he nodded. She turned and walked from the rock ledge, not looking back, but he saw the pain in her lovely face. He waited and then followed again, once more hanging back. He had followed her halfway down the slope when he suddenly saw the six near-naked riders on a trail nearby. He halted and yanked the Colt out at once. The six Shoshoni were about to cross directly in front of Dawn, and as he raised the Colt he saw the lead rider rein to a halt. The others followed his gaze and saw Dawn walking through the trees.

As one, they turned and hurried away through the trees, and Fargo dropped the Colt back into its holster. Their fear of her had been almost palpable as they fled the spirit woman. He continued to follow Dawn as she finally reached the house and went inside. She left the door open, and he wondered if only weather made her close it. He hurried past and returned to where he'd left the Ovaro in the trees. He spent the rest of the afternoon riding the mountains. He decided to follow a trail of unshod hoofprints, and he saw where they were joined by others. Marks on the ground showed that the Indians had pulled something behind them. He paused and examined the marks more carefully. They had dragged a deer carcass, he saw. They had a mountain camp somewhere, but he didn't try to find it as the shadows began to lengthen across the mountains. He turned the Ovaro back and climbed the steep mountain forests again.

The moon had risen when he reached Dawn's hideaway where a lamp from inside sent a yellow square of light into the darkness. He rode to a halt, dismounted, and she came to the door, the deep red dress replaced by a floor-length cotton robe. "Come in," she said, her direct eyes unsmiling.

"Done the rest of your thinking?" he asked.

"Not all," she said. "I know what it is you expect of me."

"What's that?" he queried.

"You expect me to say that because I was wrong about the cougar I may be wrong about Roy Coulter."

"That's plain enough now, isn't it?" Fargo said.

"Nothing is plain. Why did my good friend turn killer?" she asked. "It is plain that he did. It is not plain why."

"I don't have the kind of answers you want. Some animals turn rogue, become outlaws from their own kind. Some men do the same. We find reasons to explain men turning bad. We can't explain about animals as easily. But maybe it's not that different. Some turn while others don't. Maybe it's something inside, not outside."

"Other things stick in me. I told you, I believe everything happens for a reason. We may not know the reason, but there is one. Nothing happens for nothing," she said.

"You're not just talking about the cougar."

"No. Why did I come out to let you see me? At first I thought it was because I saw you save the woman and the child. You were not like the others who pass this way. But then I knew that was not enough. There was something more. It happened because it was meant to happen, whatever the reasons, and that's what is important. I used to hear it said that someone was feeling instead of thinking. I wonder if they're all that separate. It seems to me that feeling is thinking without all the searching."

"Pure, simple, uncomplicated."

"Maybe better."

"It can lead you astray. You just saw that."

"So can thinking."

He smiled, unable to deny the truth in her answer. "What about Roy Coulter?" he asked.

"He is not a killer," she said.

"Dammit, honey, I can't go with your feelings," Fargo said, trying to keep anger from his voice.

"I couldn't look for him at night," she said, and he nodded, happy to accept the implication in her words. "You can stay here for the night," she said.

"All right. I'd like that," he said. Her eyes searched his face, a tiny furrow touching her brow.

"I have never done this before. I have never wanted to," she said.

"It's been a bad day, a day of pain, and you're hurting inside. Maybe you just need company," he said.

"That is true and not true enough," she said, and he frowned at the remark. "See to your horse. I'll put dinner on," she said, and he went outside, unsaddled the pinto, and let the horse graze on a patch of fescue grass. He filled a bucket of water and left it for the horse and went inside again. Dawn had two plates on the table, both heaped with beets, cabbage, and turnips in a mixture of broths. There was a jar of light amber liquid beside two glasses. She poured a glass for him and for herself, and he felt his brows raise as he sipped of it.

"Applejack," he said.

"My father taught me how to make it," Dawn smiled.

"He taught you well," Fargo said, taking another sip. "Have you thought ahead?" he asked as they ate. "About the rest of your life? You don't want to become the old woman of the mountains, do you?"

"I haven't thought that far," Dawn said. "I've been happy here, continuing with my father's work, drawing and painting the birds of the mountains. I'm going to need more supplies soon, though. There is so much more to do, a lifetime of work. But it is lonely sometimes, especially the past year." She paused and smiled, an abstract, thoughtful smile. "More than lonely," she said. "Restless."

Her light blue eyes met his smile, no coyness to her, only that direct open honesty. "Could be called growing up," he offered. "There are different kinds of needing." He finished the meal and pushed back from the table and watched her rise and fold herself on the sofa. He followed and sat down beside her. "I didn't mean to upset you more," he said.

"It's just that those who have passed through these mountains have made me want never to need," she said. "And now suddenly it's all different." He watched the faint pink flush suffuse her cheeks as she kept her face to his. "You've made it all different."

"Maybe I just came by at the right time," Fargo said.

"Maybe you brought the right time," she said, her lips parted, waiting, almost a pout on their fullness. He leaned forward and gently pressed her mouth to his. He felt the hotness of her skin. Her arms slid around his neck, and she kissed him back. The honey-sweet taste of her enveloped him, willing and trusting, wanting, and giving. He felt her hand undoing the buttons of the dress. Her shoulders moved, not quite a wriggle in its grace, and then she was naked, even lovelier than she had been at the lake, all warm delicacy and deep glowing. She slid from the sofa onto a bearskin rug, and he shed his clothes as he came down beside her.

She pushed onto both knees as her eyes slowly moved over his muscled symmetry, round, blue saucers of eager interest. Once again, she was a kneeling wood nymph, all slender loveliness, a creature of fable and fantasy, delicate yet shimmering, all innocence, yet somehow all sensuality. His hands reached out and closed around the small, high breasts, so piquant and perfect for her slender body, so little-girl and so womanly at once. He caressed the delicate pink nipples, and her sigh was a sweet shuddering sound. Their flatness rose, tiny tips pushing upwards, seeking, offering.

He brought his lips down to one soft tip, drew it into his mouth, and touched the smoothness with his tongue. He caressed the edges of it and sucked gently on the tip that had grown just enough to hold between his lips. Her breath became a long gasp. "I am Dawn," she cried out. "You are fire." Her arms tightened around him. He kept his mouth on her breasts, and she shuddered little gasps as his hand moved down her warm slenderness, pressing the flat abdomen, and pausing at the tiny indentation. "Oh, my fire, my fire," she cried out as his hand moved down again, and she cried out with a moment of alarm in the sound as he pressed the thin, fuzzlike nap and felt the swell of her pubic mound.

Her slender legs were raised, held tightly together,

and she moved them from side to side. He pressed gently into the warmth between her thighs and heard her cry out as she kept her legs hard together. He moved his hand slowly along the warmth of her inner thighs, up to the dark, secret place, and he pressed his palm upward. "Oh, oh, ooooh," Dawn gasped and he felt her thighs relax, grow loose, and fall apart. He brought his hand upward at once. As he touched the tip of the fuzzlike mound, her legs lifted and kicked outward suddenly; her hands were little fists pounding into his back. He moved gently, touched one tender, quivering spot, and felt the wetness of her. "Fargo . . . oh, my fire, my flame, oh, yes, yes, yes . . ." Dawn half screamed, and her slender, long legs lifted, pressed into his sides as his hand reached deeper, caressing and stroking. She was screaming, high, eager screams, pleasure and wanting curling in each cry.

He lifted, turned, and brought his throbbing warm stiffness against her, the fuzzlike nap a strange yet exciting sensation. Dawn was holding herself against him, her long thighs raised, crying and laughing and crying as he slid slowly into her wetness. The scream became a wild paean to pleasure, and he felt her tightness around him, and he slowed and held, letting his own throbbing gently press against the honeyed wall. She was crying, he heard, yet there was only joy in the sound, a strange mixture of pleasure and pain made one, and he waited and let his throbbing gently press and expand. "Come to me, come to me, come to me." He heard Dawn's whispered moan. "All of you, all of you, I am burning, burning, sweet fire."

He plunged forward and she screamed, but the scream turned into a shout of triumph, and her thighs were opening and closing, slapping against his sides, and now her lovely nymph body rose and fell ·with him, pushed and pulled back, thrust forward again, and the cornsilk hair flew from side to side as she laughed and cried out and laughed again. "Yes, yes, oh my God, yes, yes," she managed between screams, and his wood nymph had become a writhing explosion of sensuality, all pure hedonism now, purity made of primal desire. The moment was a first for her, as new as the first sun seen by the first woman, as shining as the first morning on earth. It was indeed her own dawn, and her scream rose high as he felt her quivering around him, contractions of excruciating pleasure that swept him up with her, and he was one with her, his own voice joining her cries.

When she finally ceased quivering, the long, slender body finally curving back to fall against the rug, her cries became a whimper, and he stayed inside her as she clung to him. "Too soon, too soon," she half sobbed.

"It always is," he murmured.

"More," she whispered into his ear.

"Later," he said, and she nuzzled against him, placed his hand around one high, firm breast. "Dawn," she said. "My name has a new meaning for me, now." He smiled as the writhing, sensuous woman seemed to have vanished, and the little girl was beside him now. "So much has happened in one day," she said thoughtfully.

"That's the way of it sometimes," he said.

"I often thought, wondered, tried to imagine. It was more wonderful than anything I imagined. I know it wouldn't have been with anyone else. You made it so," she said.

"There is a time for everything," he said. "I'm glad I was part of that time." She pressed harder against him, and soon he heard her steady breathing as she fell asleep. He napped with her, but he was asleep when she woke with the dawn. He woke when he felt her hand moving across his body, and he lay still as she touched, explored, wandered. He felt her fingers touching, heard the tiny cry of delight that fell from her lips, and felt her half turn, her firm, high little breasts pressing against his stomach as she probed, touched, caressed. He also felt himself begin to respond to her exploring, and then he heard the gasp from her, surprise and then delight, and felt her fingers curl around him. She pulled, stroked, the wisdom of the flesh directing her, and she was making little sounds of delight as he reached down and cupped his hands around the high, firm, delicate pink nipples.

She swung around to him, her mouth hot against his, and as the dawn rose her cry again filled the cabin, stronger than before, a new primeval power in it, as if something deep inside her had burst free. Later, as the sun came into the room, she woke again and sat up and rubbed her eyes. She was breathtakingly lovely, that strange admixture again, girl-woman and slender forest sprite, but her little smile held a new wisdom in it. He rose, stood at the door and watched her go outside beautifully naked and wash with the well water.

"There's a towel behind the door," she said, and he brought it to her and dried her with it. She went into the house while he washed. She wore the simple straight sheath of a dress in which he had first seen her. After he finished washing, he went in to pull on clothes. She gave him wild plums on which to breakfast, and she leaned against the door as she ate. "I feel so wonderful, so new," she said dreamily.

"Wonderful enough to take me to Roy Coulter?" he asked.

"Yes," she said. "But he did not kill anyone. I want to feed the eagle before we go."

"I'll follow along behind you," Fargo said, and as she fetched the pieces of wild turkey meat he saddled the Ovaro and then followed her on foot to the rock ledge. As she had the previous time, she stood very still and alone and held her arms upward, but this time Fargo was watching the high ledges and saw the soaring form as it came into sight, gliding downward with majestic grace. He watched as the eagle circled twice over Dawn, dropping lower each time, and then suddenly it dived. But unlike the last time, the giant bird did not land at her feet with magnificent delicacy. Instead, the eagle swooped down with full force, seizing the meat with its talons and yanking it away with such power that Dawn ducked and stumbled forward. Fargo rushed into the open as she stared after the eagle as the giant bird soared away and disappeared behind a peak.

"What happened?" Fargo frowned as he helped Dawn to her feet.

"I don't know. He's never done that before," she said. "Something made him nervous, maybe another eagle came into his lair. That often happens." She shrugged, but a little frown stayed with her as they returned to the house and she got her horse, which turned out to be a smallish gray-black quarter horse. She rode bareback, he noted as he came alongside her. She led the way across the mountain. She halted along the way to watch two lynx move through the trees with light-footed steps. "I will find another Prince," Dawn remarked as they moved on.

"Have you been able to be close with any other cougar?" Fargo asked.

"Oh, yes. Two who live higher up Owl Mountain.

Of course, it will take time to bond as closely as I was with Prince. But that took time, also," she said.

"It always takes time to form a bond, to establish trust and closeness, I'm sure," Fargo said.

"Not always," Dawn said, and he caught the little private smile that crossed her face.

"That's different," he said. She laughed and put her horse into a trot along a deer trail that stayed surprisingly straight as it crossed the mountainside. The day had turned warmer, and the sun moved into the afternoon sky when she finally drew to a halt and nodded to a heavy growth of Norway spruce with a few giant Douglas firs mixed in.

"Straight through there," she said. "He lives in a hollow in the mountain, almost a cave, but not quite. He often doesn't wake till the day ends."

"Maybe it'd be best if I went in by myself," Fargo said and she thought for a moment.

"There'll be no need to hurt him," she said.

"I didn't come to do that," he said.

"Go on foot, or he'll wake and run. I'll follow behind you," Dawn said, and Fargo dismounted, draped the Ovaro's reins over a low branch, and started for the dense stand of spruce. He glanced back as he entered the trees and saw Dawn following. He moved on cautious, silent steps, keeping a straight line, and it was soon that he saw the mountainside curve inward. He spied the scattering of boxes outside the hollow, the remains of small cooking fires and clothes draped over a branch. He moved closer at a crouch and dropped to one knee as the figure suddenly stepped from deeper in the hollow. Fargo spotted the small stream a half-dozen feet to the left. Roy Coulter seemed more wild animal than human, a tremendous head of unkempt black hair and a black beard, dark, hollowed eyes and gaunt cheeks, bare torso criss-crossed with scars and torn jeans. He watched as the man knelt at the brook and drank from it with noisy, gulping sounds.

Fargo stepped forward with three long strides, one hand on the Colt at his side, though Roy Coulter seemed unarmed except for a hunting knife hung from his belt. Coulter's keen hearing caught Fargo's foot-steps and he leaped up, whirled, and stared at his visitor with his knees bent, his black, hollowed eyes carrying both fear and anger. "Who are you?" he growled in a hoarse, grating voice.

"Name's Fargo."

"How'd you get here?" Roy Coulter asked.

"I've my ways," Fargo said.

"What do you want?"

"Came to talk, about Josh Gibson."

The man's black eyes grew crafty. "Never heard the name," he said.

"I know better," Fargo said.

"Go away," Roy Coulter rasped.

"Tell me what happened to Josh Gibson," Fargo said.

"Don't know anything. Get out of here."

"You know," Fargo persisted.

Roy Coulter glared back and suddenly exploded in a sideways leap, quick and agile. He started to race for the trees and Fargo flung himself forward in a diving tackle that just managed to catch the man around the ankles. Roy Coulter went down and tried to pull away, but Fargo twisted on his right leg. The man cursed in pain. Fargo pulled him back, and yanked him to his feet. Now there was only fear in the hollowed eyes.

"You sold Josh Gibson's fancy saddle," Fargo said,

holding the man by one arm. "Did you kill him for it?"

"No, didn't kill him, didn't kill anybody," Roy Coulter said. There was a trapped animal fear in him now.

"What did you do with Josh Gibson?" Fargo pressed. He let go of the man's arm as he took a step backward. Fargo dropped one hand to his holster in emphasis. Roy Coulter's eyes darted back and forth nervously, and he seemed about to try another leap. "Don't," Fargo said. "Just tell me what happened to Josh Gibson."

Roy Coulter's eyes suddenly stopped darting and stared past him, and Fargo glanced to his right to see Dawn standing quietly. "What're you here for?" Coulter shouted at her.

"Now, calm down, Roy," Dawn said. Fargo saw the man's eyes dart to him and then back to Dawn and his face darken.

"You brought him. That's how he found me. You brought him," Roy Coulter accused and turned to Fargo. "Ask her about Josh Gibson, he shouted. "Ask her." Fargo felt the crease form on his brow as he glanced at Dawn. "She knows. She killed him," Roy Coulter shouted. "She's the one."

Fargo felt the crease become a furrow as he stared at Dawn.

6

Dawn stood absolutely still, her eyes on Roy Coulter. "Now, Roy, you know that's not the way it was," she said quietly.

Coulter shook the black mane of hair vigorously as he nodded up and down. "Yes, it was, yes it was," he shouted. "You brought him here and told him I did it."

"I didn't tell him that," Dawn said. "He wanted to talk to you himself."

"You brought him, goddamn you. Nobody comes here. You know that, and you brought him," Coulter shouted. He charged at Dawn, yanking the hunting knife from his belt as he did. "I'll show you, I'll show you," he screamed.

Fargo moved quickly. He stuck out one foot and tripped Coulter, and the man went sprawling. Fargo was on him as he rose and charged at Dawn again. Fargo's right sank deep into the man's thin torso, and Roy Coulter let out a groan of pain as he sank to the ground and rolled over, both hands clutched to his abdomen. Fargo picked up the hunting knife and tossed it aside as he watched the man shudder in pain, no more fight left in him.

"You still sure he wouldn't kill?" Fargo tossed at Dawn as she stared, wide-eyed, at Roy Coulter where he lay.

"He felt I betrayed him by bringing you," she said.

"Reasons don't count. Your second mistake. Don't try for three," Fargo said harshly. "Now, you want to tell me what exactly he meant?"

She nodded, a tiredness coming into her face, and she sank down on a piece of log. "Josh Gibson came upon me, purely by accident. I was helping Roy, bandaging his leg where he had cut it. Roy often came to me for things like that. He trusted me, just as the animals trust me. I told Josh Gibson to go away, but he wouldn't listen. He grabbed me, started to tear my dress off. I was fighting with him, and Roy couldn't help me because of his leg. Josh Gibson hit me, knocked me to the ground, and I screamed."

"The cougar came," Fargo said.

"Yes. Prince came from the trees. He attacked Josh Gibson. He would have killed him right then and there if I hadn't been able to stop him," Dawn said. "Maybe I shouldn't have."

"What's that mean?" Fargo frowned.

"Josh Gibson was so badly torn apart," she said.

"That he died of the wounds," Fargo supplied.

"No," Dawn said sadly. "He lived. I nursed him, cleaned the wounds, bandaged him, and he lived."

"He lived. So where is he?" Fargo questioned.

"I'll take you to him," she said "Let's go back and get the horses." She paused and knelt down beside Roy Coulter, who was making small, frightened sounds. "It's all right, Roy. Everything is all right," she said before she rose and went back through the trees with Fargo. "I told you he's a child," she said.

"In a man's body who was ready to kill," Fargo said coldly.

"Everything is changed suddenly," she said, frowning.

"Maybe it never was quite the way you saw it," he

told her, and she fell silent as they got the horses. She led the way down the mountainside to another trail, turning back halfway to her place before she halted and slid to the ground. She pushed a cluster of tall shrubs aside, and Fargo saw the small cave. He followed after her as she entered.

Two candles burned and lighted the cave, and he saw the figure against the wall, one arm tied to a protrusion of stone at the other end of a long rope. Fargo took in plates, a broom, a bucket of water. The small cave had been kept clean, not even an odor of dankness in it. He knew his brow was creased as he stepped to the figure. "Josh Gibson," he said. The figure didn't move, and Fargo squatted down beside it. Slowly, the man's head turned, and Fargo stared into eyes that might just as well have been lifeless. They were blank orbs that stared back at him out of a slack-jawed face that still bore the terrible scars that ran almost completely around his neck and down along the breastbone.

Josh Gibson was breathing, and as far as that went, he was alive. But he was a vegetable, without power of recognition, unable to speak, only dimly aware of anything at all, a breathing organism without thought or feeling. Fargo's thoughts unreeled to a time long ago when he had seen another man such as this. His brain had been shattered by a bullet, but he somehow had stayed alive. He'd stayed that way for years, a nothing that somehow breathed, a man dead in every respect but one, his ability to breathe.

"Jesus, how'd this happen?" Fargo said, rising to face Dawn.

"I didn't know it was happening. I was treating his wounds. I thought I was making him better," she said.

Fargo glanced at Josh Gibson, at the terrible scar

that went clear around the base of his neck. The cougar's teeth had severed the back of the spinal cord. All the while Dawn had worked to heal his wounds, no life-giving oxygen had reached his brain. All the while she had treated him his brain had been shriveling, all the while he was becoming this vegetable that breathed. Of course, she had no way of knowing that until later. But there were questions that rose in front of him, and he brought his gaze back to Dawn.

"There came a time when you had to know," he said more sternly than he'd intended. "Why didn't you try to get him down the mountain? Why didn't you try to find him a doctor?"

She put her fingers to her temples. "I was afraid. I couldn't think of anything but the terrible thing that had happened. I was afraid of men rushing up to hunt Prince, maybe take me back to jail. I didn't know what to do or what to think except that I was very afraid. As I watched him, I knew that no one could do anything for him. I decided the best thing was to keep the awful truth my own secret. It was a tragic accident, a terrible thing, but it was done. Nothing could change it, and there was no gain in having more terrible things happen because of it. But I promised myself to take care of him so long as he stayed alive, and that's what I've done."

She halted, drew herself up to stand very straight, and met his gaze. He believed every word she had said. Lying wasn't part of her. She was afraid of the outside world, and she had panicked. Perhaps not commendable, but perfectly understandable. From what he had seen and heard, two facts had become crystal clear. Josh Gibson had met with a tragic fate, and he had brought it on himself. Harsh but true. The surrounding details fell into place. Half-mad Roy

Coulter had taken Josh Gibson's saddle to the trading post to sell it. He'd done nothing more than that. He reached out and gently pulled Dawn to him. "I understand," he said.

Her cornsilk hair fell against his face as she leaned into his chest. "Thank you," she murmured.

"But there are things I must do," he said.

"What things?" she asked, alarm in her face at once.

"I must take him back to his father. I will explain everything that happened, but I must take him back," Fargo said, thinking of Bonnie waiting for her freedom.

"You must do what you think is right," Dawn said simply.

"Do you think he can ride?" Fargo asked.

"He can sit up, and he can walk," she said. "With help."

"I'll see that he stays in the saddle," Fargo said.

"I'll feed him first. I feed him twice a week. It seems enough," Dawn said. "Vegetables and water."

"I'll wait outside for you," Fargo said, and he left the cave and took a length of lariat and prepared for the long ride back. When Dawn called, he returned to the cave and lifted Josh Gibson to his feet. With Dawn helping, he half walked and half dragged the man to the Ovaro, lifted him into the saddle, and swung on behind him. He held Josh Gibson with one hand to prevent him from toppling from the horse and then wrapped the lariat around himself and his burden, tying a simple knot at the man's chest. "This way I can make time without having to go slow and hold him on," Fargo told Dawn, and she nodded as she stepped to the side of the horse.

"You will come back, won't you?" she asked. "Every-

thing has changed. It is all different now. I need you."
She paused. "I want you," she added softly.

"I'll come back, promise," he said.

"I'll wait for you," she said. "Hurry."

Tied to Josh Gibson's form, he couldn't lean down, but he let his hand hold her face for a long moment, and she understood. He sent the Ovaro on in a walk and began the long trip down the mountainside. As the trails grew steeper he was soon glad he'd thought of tying Josh Gibson to him. He'd never have been able to hold the limp figure in place otherwise, he realized. The last of the day soon melted away, and the moon rose. Fargo decided to go on through the night. He had need only to keep moving downward; there was no trail he had to follow. When he reached the bottom he'd be facing Lost Trail Pass, and he could easily find his way through there. Riding through the night was not only a practical possibility, it was emotionally attractive. Riding in the same saddle with the silent, limp form was particularly distasteful, not unlike riding with a breathing corpse.

He watched the moon as he rode, traced its slow progress across the sky, and fought away attacks of plain tiredness. Finally he moved through the deep, cavernous walls of Lost Trail Pass. He skirted Bert Drain's place. He had no reason to stop. The man had been no more than a small and unpleasant cog in a tragic wheel. The sun began to streak the sky when he was through the pass, and he kept on as the land took on shape and form. It had reached midmorning when he saw the buildings of Jim Gibson's mine appear, workmen dotting the land around the scattered mine entrances. He nosed the pinto downward and then along the road that passed Bonnie's house and led to the office.

He had just reached the building when Jim Gibson rushed out, his eyes wide, his mouth open as he stared at the figure of his son. He started to shout in joy, and the sound broke off and died away as a strangled noise. Fargo undid the length of lariat that bound Josh Gibson's form to him, eased the limp figure downward where Jim Gibson lowered his son to the ground. "Josh. Josh," the man cried out as others came from the building to gather around. Jim Gibson turned his face upward to Fargo as he cradled the silent, staring, blank form in his arms. "My God, my God, what is this? What happened to him?" he cried out, anguish in his face.

"Come inside," Fargo said, and the man motioned to some of the others looking on.

"Take him into the house, my bedroom," Gibson ordered and waited until the men were carrying the silent form away before he followed Fargo into the office.

"Tell me, goddammit, tell me," the man rasped.

"It was a tragedy, all of it, one terrible thing piled onto another," Fargo said.

"Give it to me, everything you found out," Gibson demanded, and Fargo told him how it began and how it had ended. He left out no details, and when he finished he saw nothing but a terrible fury in the man's face. "That bitch. That goddamn crazy bitch. She's going to pay for this," Gibson thundered.

"That cat sprang to protect her. It was all a matter of natural reactions. It wasn't her doing," Fargo said.

"The hell it wasn't. The goddamn cat was her pet. She'd no business letting it near people. Only a crazy woman keeps a damn cougar as a pet," Gibson raged.

"She tried to save Josh. She was the one who kept him alive all these months," Fargo said.

"Alive? Alive? My son's not alive. He's as good as dead, and she's the reason for it. She killed him," Gibson snarled as the four men entered the office.

"He's on your bed, boss. Shall we go get the doc?" one asked.

"The doc won't help Josh," Gibson said. "Nothing will help him, but I'm going to see that he gets his revenge."

"You mean your revenge," Fargo said.

"I mean payment for killing my boy," Gibson roared.

The man was emotionally out of control. All the months of waiting and hoping and now this terrible end. The cruelty of truth was perhaps the only way to reach him, Fargo saw. "Josh brought it on himself," Fargo said and saw Gibson recoil as if he'd been physically struck. "He attacked her. None of it would've happened if he hadn't done that. I know those are hard words, but that's the truth of it."

Gibson's rage remained as his face grew dark. "The truth is normal women don't have goddamn cougars there to tear a man apart. The truth is you've no grounds defending that wild bitch."

"I'm not defending. I'm telling you how, what, and why. Take care of your son. There's no need for accusing. There's no need for anything but accepting the truth," Fargo said.

"There's need, goddammit. There's need to make her pay for this," Gibson said.

Fargo's lips tightened. The man couldn't accept reason. Grief had twisted his mind. He was beyond thinking clearly, unable to come to grips with his son's role in the tragedy. Rage and the thirst for punishment were his way of refusing to face the truth. "I can't let

110

you do that, Gibson. That'd be very wrong," Fargo said.

"You've nothin' more to do with it," Gibson said and went for his gun. Fargo's Colt was in his hand at once, but he saw the other men had drawn, also. "You'll get me, but not all of us," Gibson said.

"I'll get three of you at least," Fargo said.

"Not before you're blasted," Gibson said, and Fargo swore silently at the reality of the remark. It was all too close. Some of their shots had to find their mark. "I don't want this, Fargo. You did your job. You earned your pay. Give me your gun, and leave the rest to me. Soon as it's over you can go your way alive," Gibson said.

Fargo's thoughts were racing. The odds were too stacked against him. He had to buy time. "What about Bonnie? She was part of our bargain," he said.

"She goes back to her place and her job soon as you hand me your gun," Gibson said. Fargo nodded and pushed the Colt at him. Gibson took it and motioned to his men. "Take him. Tie him up good," he said. Fargo stood still as the men pulled his arms behind him. He felt his wrists being bound. "Just so's you don't get any ideas of trying to get away and warn her we're coming," Gibson said. "When I get back you can go your way."

He turned, whispered orders to his men, and strode from the office. The men let some ten minutes go by before they marched Fargo from the office, around the building, and back into the hills, past a storage shack and another shack. They halted at a shed set behind a low hill and pushed him into a neat room. There was a lamp burning inside, and Fargo saw a cot, a small table, and a chair. One high window afforded daylight, and he saw the door was sturdy, a heavy bolt on the outside. Obviously obeying orders, the men trussed his ankles together and let him hop to the cot where he half fell onto it.

"You'll get your hands untied while you eat," the one said. "There'll be two guards outside day and night. You need something you holler. Just don't make trouble."

"Wouldn't think of it," Fargo said and watched the men leave. He heard the bolt slide into place as he lay down on the cot. He felt his nostrils twitch as he picked up the scent. This was where they'd kept Bonnie. Gibson had just taken her out while his men waited in the office. Fargo drew his knees up as he rolled onto his side and tried to reach the throwing knife in its calf holster. He swore as the ropes around his wrists kept him from reaching low enough to pull his trouser leg up. Straightening out, he lay back and toyed with other plans. He had a small cushion of time. Gibson wouldn't find Dawn quickly. There was a chance he wouldn't find her at all, but that was a chance he couldn't risk taking, Fargo knew. The man was on a mission. He'd search with hate and determination.

Fargo grimaced and stretched his shoulder muscles. He'd have to find the right moment, even if it meant waiting longer. He couldn't help Dawn by getting himself shot. He closed his eyes and let the hours go by with infuriating slowness. The little high window told him that night had fallen. He finally heard the bolt being slid open, and he swung his legs from the cot. The four men entered, one carrying a tray of cold beef and potato, the other three with their guns drawn. The man set the tray on the small table, brought it in front of Fargo and untied his hands. Fargo rubbed his wrists before setting to the dinner as his quick glances showed him the other three men were lined up against the far wall, all with guns in hand.

They had plainly been instructed to take no chances. They were tense, very on guard. They'd be less so next time and still less so the time after. He'd have to wait, watch, perhaps make his own moment. This wasn't it, he realized and finished the meal. "A man has to take care of more than his stomach," he said as the man pulled the tray and table away.

"Outside," one of the others said. "Untie his legs." Fargo sat quietly as the ankle bonds were undone, and they led him outside to an outhouse, let him enter, and stood back with guns aimed at the door. When he emerged they tied his wrists behind him again. "How about a little looser?" he said.

"Like hell," the one said as he was marched back into the room and his ankles were bound together again. The men left, and Fargo rolled onto the couch, his eyes narrowed in thought, the beginning of a plan forming. In the outhouse he had both ankles and wrists unbound. It seemed the best chance he'd have, but it was hardly a good one, he swore inwardly. He'd have to be very fast and very lucky, and he disliked depending on luck. He closed his eyes, turned over thoughts and plans. He was unhappy with all of them, and he finally fell asleep. The night wore on in silence.

He slept uncomfortably, bound hand and foot as he was, and finally woke as the morning sun slanted through the small, high window. He called the guards, and they let him go to the outhouse, once again with four of them waiting. But this time, with his hands untied, he took the knife from its calf holster and put it inside his shirt, tucked it into his belt deep enough so that most of it extended down against his left leg. He held his breath when they tied his hands behind him again and then, when he was back in the hut, his ankles. "When's breakfast?" he asked. "Never knew a man could get so hungry just being tied up."

"In a half hour," one of the men answered as he closed the door and put on the bolt. Fargo stayed quietly on the couch. He'd found out what he wanted to know. He wouldn't try to get to the knife. It could take time, and he didn't want them walking in on him with breakfast just as he had the knife freed. He lay back and waited, reassured by the touch of the steel against his leg. When they returned with breakfast, one untied his hands again and the other three stood with guns drawn against the wall while he ate.

His wrists were bound behind him again when he finished. They left, and Fargo drew a deep sigh. They hadn't detected the thin blade, and he swung his legs over the edge of the cot and stood up. He began to hop straight up and down, staying at it until he felt the knife dislodge from inside his belt and slide down his trouser leg. He halted and fell back onto the cot as the blade landed on the floor. Turning his back, he began to squat down and feel for the knife. He had only to grope for a minute before his fingers found the cold steel and moved to curl around the hilt.

Working slowly, barely able to hold the knife between his fingers, he turned the double-edged blade upward and began to make little sawing motions against the wrist ropes. In less than fifteen minutes he found he had to stop, his fingers cramped and his wrist muscles aching. He hadn't enough slack to make but the tiniest of swing motions, and he couldn't really bring any pressure to bear on the ropes. He realized it was uncertain whether he'd be able to cut his bonds at all, but it'd plainly take a day or longer. His cramped fingers relaxed enough so he could start sawing again when he heard the voices just outside the door. "Damn," he swore. He bent down, dropped the knife on the floor, and using both his bound-together feet, he pushed the knife under the cot just as the door opened. Bonnie stepped in with one of the guards, still arguing.

"Jim told me I could visit," she said.

"He didn't say anything to me about him having visitors. Not to any of the others, either," the man said.

"It's all right, you can ask him yourself when he gets back," Bonnie insisted. The man stayed against the door he closed as Bonnie took a pair of steps toward Fargo and then turned to frown at the guard. "I'd like to be alone, if you don't mind," she said.

"I mind, dammit. I'm not sure you ought to be visitin' at all," the man said. "I think you'd better leave."

"I just got here, Jake," Bonnie said and stepped to where Fargo sat on the edge of the cot. "I saw Josh. What happened. Jim didn't say anything when he let me loose." He told her quickly, and she grimaced when he finished. "How awful. A real tragedy," she said.

"Only your friend can't understand that. He wants revenge because it'll make him feel better," Fargo said, and Bonnie nodded.

"I suspected as much. I told you, he's become a changed man because of this. He can't think straight anymore," she said. Then her face suddenly broke into an almost dreamy smile. "You remember Utah and Banker Jethroe, of course," she said, and Fargo nodded. "Well, I always say turn about is fair play," Bonnie added, and, her back to the man at the door, she reached deep inside her blouse, and when her hand came out Fargo saw it had his Colt in it. She spun and faced the guard with the revolver aimed at him as she walked toward him. "Sorry about this Jake, but I'll take your gun," she said.

"Dammit, Bonnie," the man protested, but Bonnie held her hand out.

"Now, Jake. Take it out nice and slow. I don't want to shoot you by accident," Bonnie said, and the man did as she intructed, carefully handing her his gun. "Now lay down on your stomach, Jake," she said, and the man obeyed again.

"Sam and the others are right outside," he said.

"I know that, Jake," Bonnie said as she backed to where Fargo sat, and keeping the Colt trained on the man, she began to untie the wrist ropes with one hand.

"There's a knife under the cot. Use it. It'll be faster," he said, and she allowed a small giggle of surprise.

"Might have known you weren't just sitting around," she said.

"I wasn't getting far. I'm sure glad to see you," he told her as she found the knife and quickly severed the wrist ropes. He took the Colt as she cut his ankle bonds, and he rose to his feet. "Where'd you get my Colt?" he asked.

"I stopped at Jim's office. I expected he put it there, and I was right," Bonnie said, and Fargo crossed to the closed door in three long-legged strides.

"Get up," he ordered the man, who pushed himself to his feet. "You call the others in," Fargo said. "I'm not Bonnie. I won't be shooting you by accident. One wrong move and you're dead on purpose."

He placed himself behind the door as he pulled it open, and the man called out. "Better come in here,"

Jake said and stepped back, casting a quick, nervous glance at the Colt still trained on him. The three other men hurried into the room, and Fargo pressed the Colt against the back of Jake's neck.

"Drop your guns. I don't want to shoot him, but I'm not going to stand still for something wrong," Fargo said. The trio hesitated, but decided to obey. They let their six-guns drop to the floor, where Bonnie scooped them up while Fargo pushed Jake over to where the others were standing. "Now, that's acting real sensible," Fargo said. "More so than your boss. How many men did he take with him?"

"Ten," one of the others said.

Fargo motioned for Bonnie to step outside before him, and then he followed, pulled the door shut, and slipped the bolt on. "Somebody will stop by later and let them out," Fargo said as he hurried across the ground to the stable with Bonnie. She watched as he saddled the horse.

"Good luck, Fargo. I hope you can stop this before more harm's done," she said. "Come back if you can."

"If I can," he said, and Bonnie clung to him for a moment before stepping back to let him swing onto the Ovaro. He waved back as he rode northward, his eyes sweeping the ground. It was easy enough to pick up the trail of the ten horsemen. They had ridden straight north into the mountains, and he followed until the day wore to an end and the night ruled out further tracking. When daylight came he was in the saddle, following the hoofprints again. Gibson had led his men high into Owl Mountain and directly on a path toward Dawn's place. Pure luck had put him on his path, Fargo knew, and he saw where Gibson had dispatched four riders in different directions to form a net of searchers.

He slowed as he let his outriders beat their way through the heavy mountain forests, and he paused more often to rest his horses, Fargo saw in the tracks. He still had a good distance to go before nearing where Dawn had her mountain hideaway, but the man was persisting, staying in the generally right direction as he continued to send out relays of searchers. His outriders combed the trees for a quarter of a mile on each side of the main body of Gibson's men, then circled back to rejoin the others. Gibson had slowed still more, sending out more searchers in a loose net, and Fargo came upon a small flat high plateau where the outriders all rejoined the main force, their tracks moving in from both sides.

They had moved halfway across the small high plateau when disaster struck. Fargo reined up at the first sign, the two bodies lying close to each other, each riddled with arrows. His glance instantly swept the ground, and he saw the unshod Indian pony prints that swept down from both sides of the plateau. They had streamed out of the thick mountain forests, at least twenty of them, he estimated by the number of hoofprints. He walked the Ovaro slowly forward and spied the third body a dozen yards on. Fargo dismounted and stepped to the slain man and peered at the four arrows protruding from his torso. All carried the Northern Shoshoni markings. He peered at the man's face and saw the startled expression there. He'd never had a chance to do more than be surprised.

Fargo's eyes narrowed as he studied the hoofprints that covered the scene, all still fresh. The attack hadn't occurred more than eight or ten hours earlier, he guessed, and he walked forward, letting the hoofprints form what had happened, each of them a word to his trailsman's eye, all forming sentences and then paragraphs. Gibson and his men had been ambushed. They'd hardly had a chance to fight back, and the rest of them had been taken prisoner. A line of deep prints with clearly defined edges made by horseshoes moved on toward the end of the plateau. The line was bordered by rows of unshod pony prints on both sides. Fargo climbed onto the Ovaro and followed. The Shoshoni had herded Gibson and his remaining six men to the end of the plateau where, as dusk began to slide over the mountains, he saw the hoofprints move down a slope of Norway spruce. They had taken their captives to their camp, and Fargo followed the prints, hurrying the Ovaro in the fast-fading light.

The Shoshoni had moved through the spruce as it leveled off on a wide moose path alongside the steep slope of a mountain ledge, on deeper, keeping their captives between them. The dusk began to turn to darkness, but the Indians had been moving in a steady, almost straight line, and Fargo continued to move in the same direction when he could no longer see the hoofprints. He had ridden perhaps another fifteen minutes when his nostrils picked up the scent of wood smoke, and he hurried the Ovaro until he caught the flickering light of campfires. He slowed again at once, moved forward carefully, and listened to the sound of Shoshoni voices, animated sounds as they told others of their exploits. Fargo moved another dozen yards closer. He could make out the camp. Set in an oblong sweep, there were at least five teepees, and he saw a main campfire and a smaller one off to the side. He slid from the Ovaro and crept forward on foot.

His eyes swept the trees that lined the camp, but

there were no sentries. The Shoshoni felt completely secure in their mountain camp. He crept further, almost to the edge of the trees, and halted on one knee. Gibson and his men were bound hand and foot, two to a stake, almost back to back. Gibson had a stake to himself. Fargo's eyes scanned the camp. Gibson's horses were tethered at the far end of the campsite, in a cluster, near but not mixed in with the Indian ponies. Fargo scanned the captives again. Two men bled from wounds, one a thigh wound, the other a shoulder wound. Gibson was unharmed except for a red welt across his forehead, probably caused by the side of a tomahawk, Fargo guessed. He settled down and watched and saw a number of squaws bring food to the braves around the main fire. At the teepees, he saw a half-dozen naked children still awake.

The Shoshoni were plainly in no hurry to torture or kill their captives. This night would be spent bragging about the successful capture. When enough boasting had been done they'd sleep, and when the day came, the squaws would have the privilege of getting their captives ready for their fate. That alone was usually more than most men would wish to undergo. The squaws had their own brand of cruelty. Much of it entirely impersonal, part of an ancient ritual of testing the bravery of a captive which, come night, the men would carry on with greater refinement. Impersonal or not, the end was the same—pain and death—and Fargo's eyes swept the Shoshoni camp again. The spruce led to the very edge of the far end of the oblong site, and as he watched and waited, the squaws and children began to retire into their teepees. As the moon rose high, the men finally ended their boasting and storytelling and began to prepare for the night.

Many went into teepees, one in particular, a tall

brave with a bear-claw earring who appeared to be the leader. But too damned many stretched out on the ground, some wrapping themselves in blankets, and slept, most in a long line that fronted the edge of the site. Fargo's eyes surveyed the camp again, and he swore inwardly. There might have been a chance if most of the braves had retired into teepees, but that hadn't happened. He couldn't see any way to free Gibson and the others. He might be able to sneak in and free one man, Gibson, and crawl away, but seven men crawling away would surely wake the Shoshoni. He thought of trying to crawl in and free each one at a time, and almost as quickly cast aside the thought. He'd be stretching luck to be able to make one trip into the camp and get out without waking anyone. These braves had not gotten themselves drunk on jimsonweed. They'd be quick to wake at the slightest sound.

Damn the man, Fargo swore. It was almost a pattern of self-destruction. The son had triggered his tragedy by attacking Dawn, and now the father had done much the same. There was no way he could free Gibson and his men with the Shoshoni there. Most of the braves would have to leave the camp for him to have any chance, and that wouldn't be happening, he knew and he felt the utter helplessness sweep over him. But as he stared at the sleeping camp the impossible solution kept stabbing at him. The Shoshoni had to leave their camp for him to have any chance at rescuing Gibson. And they had to leave quickly, in haste or alarm, without time to slay their captives first. The impossible was becoming more impossible.

Or was it? His lips drew back in a grimace. As sometimes happened, maybe the events themselves held the seeds of their own solution. He felt a spiral of hope forming inside himself as stray thoughts began to take shape. Yes, he heard himself say silently. Dammit, that was it, the only chance, the one, single chance, and it was made of a kind of bitter irony. Slowly, he began to pull backward from the edge of the Shoshoni camp.

7

Fargo silently made his way back to the Ovaro and led the horse through the dark forest for another hundred yards before he climbed into the saddle. A half-moon had risen that afforded some light as he rode up the steep mountain trail. He kept moving northward, and the night wore into the deep hours when he halted and lay down under a big lodgepole pine. Exhausted, he let himself sleep for a few hours, and then he rode northward again. As the dawn rose he brought his bearings into focus as he scanned the upper terrain of Owl Mountain. He turned onto a side trail, and the sun had cleared the high peaks when he found the dense Norway spruce mountainside that marked Dawn's hideaway.

She was outside, sitting with a pencil and a sketch-pad when he neared. She rose at the sound of the horse. She was beautifully slender in the simple dress, the yellow cornsilk hair streaming in the morning's soft, warm breeze. He swung to the ground, and she was in his arms instantly, clinging to him with a wordless embrace until he finally pulled back to peer into the light blue orbs. "I was afraid you wouldn't come back. I've never been afraid like that before. This is all so new to me," she said. "Did you take him home?"

"Yes," he told her. "And now there's something I want you to do for me."

"Anything," Dawn said and pressed her soft lips on his. The sweet-honey taste of her was wonderfully delicate. When she pulled away he told her what Josh Gibson had done and what he had gotten himself into. He wondered for a moment whether she would rebel against trying to help a man who'd come looking to kill her, but the thought had been unworthy, he realized as she answered. She was still too pure and unspoiled for that kind of response. "I'll get my horse," she said, and he waited and climbed into the saddle as she came from the rear of the house on the gray-black quarter horse. She rode beside him as he started down the mountain. They passed a quartet of white-tailed deer, and he saw Dawn's tiny frown. "They've refused to come and eat from my hand as they always have," she said. "So have the fox and the martens. Something has made them all nervous. I wish I knew what it was. Maybe a storm coming. They sense so much so easily."

"Yes, they do," Fargo said and knew, in an undefined way, that he wanted to say no more. He led the way down the mountainsides, Dawn completely happy to ride in silence beside him. The sun had moved into the later afternoon when he crossed the small plateau, still covered with the Shoshoni hoofprints, and rode down the trail that led to the wide moose path through the thick Norway spruce. They were just nearing sight of the camp when he heard the high shouts of the squaws and then a scream of pain from one of Gibson's men. He halted, slid to the ground, and Dawn did the same as he took the rifle from its saddle case and moved toward the camp, which was now clearly visible through the trees.

124

Gibson and his men were exactly as he had left them, bound to the stakes, but three of them were stripped bare; the others still with their trousers on. All showed signs of having been whipped by the thin, narrow interwoven strands of young branches the squaws fashioned into whips. Fargo glanced at Dawn. "You know what to do," he said, and she nodded. "I'll be right behind you," he said. She smiled at him with a serenity he didn't share at all. She walked forward, and he followed for another half-dozen steps, then dropped to the ground on his stomach, the rifle at his shoulder ready to fire. His eyes went to the Shoshoni camp as Dawn stepped from the trees and halted, standing tall and silent, her arms slowly lifting toward the sky.

The gasp echoed from the camp as the Indians suddenly saw her, and Fargo saw them recoil and start to fall backward, some gathering up squaws and children. She took another step forward, her arms extended fully now. The Shoshoni were running, braves, squaws, and children, some leaping onto their ponies, others fleeing into the forest on foot. It was happening just as Fargo had hoped it would, their fear of the spirit woman erupting, feeding on itself as they panicked. He stayed in place as the Shoshoni vanished into the thick forest, and he could hear the sounds of the hoofbeats in the distance. He rose and ran forward as Dawn halted and dropped her arms to her sides. He brushed past her and dropped to one knee beside Gibson. "Get the others untied," he said as he cut the man's ropes and went to the next figure.

"We weren't watching. I was thinking about the damn woman, and they hit us from both sides," Gibson said as he helped free the others. He turned to stare at Dawn as his men pulled on their clothes. "That's her, isn't it?" he breathed.

Fargo nodded. "She was the only way I could think of to save your necks," Fargo said as Gibson continued to stare at Dawn's motionless figure. "You've nothing to say to her. You never did," Fargo murmured. "Get your horses and hightail it out of here."

Gibson stared for a minute longer and then nodded as he rose to his feet and walked with his men to where the horses were tethered. Fargo saw the blanket settle over Jim Gibson, not just weariness, not just despondency, but a man coming to terms with hard truth. Gibson climbed onto his horse and rode away with the others, not looking back, and Fargo waited till they were out of sight in the gathering dusk before he turned to Dawn. "Let's go," he said. "The Shoshoni will come back. This is their camp. They've left all their things here. They'll force themselves to come back. We don't want to be here when they do. Your magic worked. Let's keep it that way."

She hurried beside him to the horses and rode at his side as he led the way out of the heavy spruce forest. They started up the mountainside as night descended. "Let's keep going till we reach my place," she said.

"Afraid of being alone in the dark in this part of the mountain?" he smiled.

"I've never been afraid of being alone in any part of the mountain night or day," Dawn said with just a hint of defensiveness. The moon rose, and they found the way together, she leading in some places, he in others. The night was nearing an end when they reached her place. She led him inside and lighted a lone candle in her bedroom. It cast a flickering glow. She turned to him as she removed her dress. He stared at the slender beauty of her wood-sprite body, the long, willowy shape, the small yet perfect high, firm breasts with their delicate pink tips, everything about her still the child-woman. "It's not fair," Dawn said.

"What's not fair?"

"I've waited for you to return, for this moment to come again, and I'm so tired," she said.

"It's fair. I'm damn tired, too," Fargo smiled as he pulled off his clothes. He lay back on the simple bed, and she came into his arms. "We'll make it up tomorrow," he said, and she nodded, smiled happily, and folded herself against him. She was asleep in minutes, perfectly content, and he let his own tiredness sweep him into slumber. He stayed asleep after the first morning sun. When he finally woke he watched Dawn open her eyes, the cornsilk hair a yellow halo around her head. He rose, went to the well outside, and refreshed himself. She joined him, beautifully naked, looking as natural as the doe that bounded past. The new sun was already hot, and she poured a bucket of well water over herself and led him back into the house. She stretched out on the bed, tiny droplets of water still glistening around the delicate pink tips of each sweet breast.

Her arms reached out for him, pulled his face down to her, and pushed one small breast into his mouth. She groaned in delight as he gently caressed it with his tongue, pulled on it, kissed its warmth. Her hands moved across his body, no tentative exploring this time, but an eager groping, a haste born of newfound desire, of pleasures tasted and hunger unleashed. "Oh, yes, yes, ooooh, yes," Dawn breathed as her hands found his throbbing warmth, and her long, slender thighs fell open at once. "Come, come, my fire, my flame, oh, yes . . . yes . . . yeeeessss," she screamed and drew him to her. He felt her open for him, enveloping, warm, moist welcome, no caution, now, only the insistence of flesh to flesh, touch to touch, sensations embracing each other until they were one.

Her wood-sprite body became a thing of shimmering ecstasy as she turned and twisted, rose and fell. She arched her back and let her long, slender thighs rub up and down against him. Yet with it all, there was no grossness in her ardor, everything brought with it a passion that never deserted delicacy. Even her words, gasped out as he slid back and forth with intensifying pleasure, possessed her own very individual naturalness. "Oh, love . . . fire . . . flame . . . oh, yes, yes . . . sweet flame . . . sweet touch . . . aaaaaah . . . aaaaah . . . yes, yes, again, oh, please again . . . so wonderful . . . so wonderful." When he felt her suddenly leap upward against him, the fuzzlike little nap pressing into him, and her nectared enclosure tightening, he came with her in delirious explosions. She screamed with pure joy, and the quivering moment was a world of itself.

She clung to him as her cry finally trailed off in a half sob, and the slender thighs stayed clasped around him, unwilling to release his inner embrace. When at last she lowered her legs and stretched out, he lay beside her, his eyes taking in the sweet beauty of her, and her hand came up to gently stroke his face. "It was everything I remembered and more," she said, and for the first time since he'd first seen her a very womanly wisdom tinged her little smile. She rose up on one elbow, the small, sweet breasts lifting with their pink-tipped delicacy to gently touch his chest. "I feel so different, so wonderfully different. Everything I feel inside me is new, changed, and it's as if I'm looking at the world with new eyes," she said.

"You are," he smiled.

"Wonderful, warm new eyes," she said dreamily and swung her lovely willowy body from the bed, rose, and slipped the simple dress on and stepped from the house. Fargo rose and pulled on his trousers and went to the doorway. She stood in the clearing, yellow hair hanging loosely down her back, and he saw the birds flutter and swoop all around her, coming down close and then winging away, all setting up a noisy chatter. He saw orioles and robins, yellow warblers and black-topped chickadees, tree swallows snd horned larks; it was a small convention of songbirds, and he watched until finally Dawn turned and came back to the house. A frown creased her brow as she took his hand. "None of them came down," she murmured.

"What do you mean?" he asked.

"They usually land on my shoulders, my head, my arms, at my feet. But they only flew all around. I don't understand it. Maybe whatever's bothering the deer and the foxes is bothering them," she said and sat down on the sofa.

"You said maybe they sense a storm or something," he reminded her as she sat with the furrow deepening on her brow.

"I know, but I don't feel a storm. I can feel those things almost as quickly as they can," Dawn said. "I wonder if it has to do with Prince."

"The cougar?" Fargo echoed.

"Yes. He was strength. Every animal respects the cougar. When he came to me the others knew. They saw him trust, and they trusted. Then they came to me," she said.

"You really believe that?" Fargo questioned.

"Yes. They understand, they exchange. There are so many ways to talk without words. We are the ones who don't understand that," Dawn said. "And maybe, in some way, they know he turned away, turned outlaw as you put it. Maybe they're not sure of me anymore, now. I'm not sure of myself, really. I'm still trying to understand Prince."

"There's nothing to understand. It happens, that's all. They are, after all, wild creatures, all of them," Fargo said and drew a glance of immediate disapproval.

"They are not wild. They are their own masters. There is a difference between wild and untamed. None of them has ever harmed me. None of them has ever been afraid of me, not cougar, eagle, or squirrel. I do not want to lose that friendship, that special thing I've had. Yes, it has to do with Prince, with the trust they saw him give. I'm more and more sure of it," she said.

He listened, and something inside him wanted to disagree, yet he couldn't find the words. He wondered if indeed he had the right to disagree. She had proven her way with the wild creatures. He had seen the miracles of relationship he would not have thought possible. Yet her explanations were not enough, he sensed. Something more was wrong, something he had still to define.

"I'd think about it some more," he suggested and saw her jaw stiffen.

"I don't have to think more about it," she said. "I'll fix it. I know how."

"What's that mean?" Fargo frowned.

"There's a cougar, higher on the mountain. I've seen him. I'll go to him, bring him down with me. The others will see then. They'll know everything is all right again," she said.

"No, you can't do that," Fargo said. "Don't try."

"Why not? Why can't I?" Dawn frowned.

He rummaged through his mind for answers that

refused to come. "I don't know, but I don't want you to try," he said. "I've got to think more about it. I just know you can't go."

"Can't?" she repeated, an edge in her voice he had never heard before.

"Sorry. Shouldn't," he said, and she let her face soften.

"But I should. I must," she said.

He rose and took her hands in his. "No, don't. I don't have the reasons now, not that I can put into words. But I know you shouldn't," he said. She leaned forward, and her lips pressed his, soft warmth. "I'll fix dinner," she said, stepping back. "You feed the horses."

He nodded and went outside to the small bin of specially grown oats she kept. He went over the Ovaro and her horse with a sweat scraper and then fed each a bag of oats. The day had begun to slide into darkness when he returned to the house, where Dawn had the table set with two plates and two tin mugs, hers already filled. She served a dish of camas root, seasoned well with wild onion, with peas and spinach and filled his mug almost to the brim. "Honey tea," she said, and he took a sip.

"Very tasty," he said.

"To us," she said, lifting her own mug, and he took a deep drink of his. "This is as good a time as any to ask," she said as they ate.

"Ask what?" he returned.

"About your staying. You know that's what I want, of course," she said.

"I can't stay. Others are waiting for me," he said.

"Will you come back?" she asked, her eyes wide.

"I'll try. I'd like to," he told her as he drank again of the tasty honey tea. No placating words. She was a very different, totally unique creature who might have stepped from the pages of a fairy tale. She proved that again when they finished eating and she lay with him in the bed, sensuous sweetness, quiet fire. He slept soundly later, holding her in his arms, and he didn't wake until the room was flooded with sunlight.

He sat up and frowned, feeling strangely tired and saw that he was alone. "Dawn?" he called out to the open door of the house, but there was no answer. He donned trousers and stepped outside and saw only a pair of deer bound away. He returned to the bedroom, the frown creeping over his brow. He was alone, and he turned and strode into the other room where they had had dinner. The table was still set, and he stared at his empty mug as the thoughts took shape inside him. He hadn't spent the day before in hard riding. There was no reason for him to have slept this late. Or was there, he growled and strode to the wood table with the two drawers.

He rummaged through the first one, then the second, and found the small jar, opened it up, and sniffed the contents. "Powdered primrose flowers," he muttered. "Used as a sedative for centuries, odorless and tasteless when mixed with something else." He dropped the jar into the drawer and strode to the bed. Her side still held warmth to his touch. She'd waited till daylight to leave, which meant she hadn't much more than three hours start on him. Damn her sweet, stubborn hide, he swore as he dressed. She was determined to prove him wrong. Or perhaps more determined to prove something to herself. Only she wouldn't, he knew without knowing why for certain. Only that she was walking into death.

He ran from the house, turned the corner, and saw

she hadn't taken the horse, for obvious reasons. She intended the cougar to return at her side. He'd no such ambitions and no reason not to take the Ovaro, and he saddled the horse and raced from the little clearing, his eyes sweeping the ground. He picked up her footprints quickly enough as she climbed upward. She was interested in speed, not masking her tracks, and he had no trouble following. He reined up at a mountain stream and saw where she had halted, shed clothes, and washed, and he nodded in grim understanding. She wanted no scent but her own on her when she met the big cat.

But she had taken close to a half hour, he guessed, and he put the Ovaro into motion again. He had gained at least an hour, perhaps close to two, between the speed of the Ovaro and the time she had spent at the stream. He had just allowed himself to hope that he might catch up to her before she reached the cougar's territory when he saw her footprints turn and climb up a narrow path on a slope too steep for the Ovaro to negotiate. Made by water coursing down the mountainside during storms, the path led upward through Sitka spruce and Douglas fir, and Fargo swung from the horse, took the big Sharps from its saddle case, and draped the reins over a low branch.

The rifle in hand, he began to pull himself up the steep pathway. He found that it led almost straight until the slope abruptly leveled off, and then it turned and soon vanished where the land grew flat enough for the rainwater to spread across it. The spruce stayed thick as he followed her prints along the relatively level land, and then, as the trail turned, he saw the trees thin out and the mountain become open space with red clay rock formations. It was the terrain favored by the big cats. They could lie motionless atop the rocks and survey everything that went on below and around them. On the rocks they had no need to concern themselves with the rustle of leaves. They could move with absolute silence on their padded paws to pounce on their completely unaware prey.

Dawn's footsteps led between two boulders, and Fargo hurried after them. He had almost reached the end of the short passage when he heard the sound of the cougar, a combination hiss and roar. He swore silently as he dropped to a crouch and ran forward out of the space between the boulders to see a wide expanse of rock with high boulders rising along one edge. Dawn was standing near the high boulders, and his eyes went to the cougar where it crouched facing her. She was making soft, soothing sounds as she slowly walked toward the big cat. There was no fear in her voice. There wouldn't be, he reminded himself. She had done this before. She had proven her gift to bond with the wild creatures, the creatures she refused to call wild.

Only it was different now. She didn't know that, didn't feel it, recognize it, understand it. Neither did he, but he knew it was there, and his eyes went to the cougar. The big cat's amber eyes were lighted, their pupils almost vertical slits, and the black-tipped tail twitched furiously. To Dawn they were only defensive signs, indications of its own fears and uncertainties. She would dispel them by her own offering of trust. After all, she had done it so often with so many. Fargo swore inwardly again as he raised the rifle to his shoulder. He could put a shot into the cougar's head, but he held back. Dawn would hate him with undying bitterness. To kill must be only to survive in her eyes, even then only if absolutely necessary. That moment of survival had still not come. The cougar still crouched, ready to spring, yet it hadn't.

She would never be convinced, Fargo realized, until that moment came, exploded in her face, beyond disbelieving once and for all, and so he waited, his finger resting against the trigger of the rifle. He played a dangerous game with Dawn's life, he realized, yet her life had been based on that special trust. To kill too quickly would be to kill a part of her, also. His lips were pulled back in a grimace of apprehension and tension as she moved toward the cougar again, stretching out both arms. He had used a fraction of a second to watch her, and the big cat chose that instant to attack. Fargo heard its low, rumbling roar as he snapped his eyes back to the rifle sight. He fired as Dawn's half-scream shattered the air, but the cougar had swerved as it charged, and his first shot grazed the animal's shoulder. His second shot was low into the ground as Dawn twisted away, almost into his path of fire.

The bullet sent up a shower of rock chips, and Fargo saw the cougar spin away, leap onto the nearest boulder, and disappear over the top. Dawn had fallen, yellow hair in disarray around her face, and she brushed it back as Fargo ran toward her. Reaching her, he pulled her to her feet with one hand. His eyes swept the boulders as the cougar let out a scream of hate and fury. "Stay with me," Fargo said as he began to back across the rock-floored open area, the rifle raised, ready to fire the moment a tawny form appeared atop the boulders. But the cougar was as clever and wily as its reputation and let him hear only its hisses as he moved behind the rocks. He continued to back up through the small chasm between the tall rock formations. The Sitka spruce forest was only a few yards away now, and he hurried toward it, no longer slowly backing away, and he halted when they had gone a dozen yards into the trees.

He turned to Dawn and saw the shock still clutching her face. "He was going to kill," she breathed. "I saw it in his eyes just as he leaped."

"Yes," Fargo said softly.

"Why? I've been with him before, stroked his body, had him rub against my leg. Why? Why? I don't understand," she said.

She was more than shaken, he saw. She was wounded, all she believed in torn from her. "We can't talk here. Let's wait till we get back to your place," he said, aware that he still had to marshal his own thoughts. She nodded, her eyes still round with shock, and she stayed at his side as he started through the forest. The sun that filtered through the trees was in the midafternoon sky, he noted, and he hurried. He wanted to be back at her place by the time night descended.

She walked in silence with him as he retraced his steps, and finally he reached the very steep, narrow rainwater runoff he had climbed up after her footprints. Dawn was as at home in the forest as any living creature, and he'd no need to tell her how to negotiate the steep downward path. She went first, using the low branches of the trees and the ends of wiry mountain shrub to slow her descent. He did the same as he followed, hanging on to keep his feet from slipping on the narrow, precipitous pathway. They were a little more than halfway down it when Fargo's ears caught the sudden sound to his left, inside the trees, a small stone suddenly knocked loose and rolling downhill.

He spun, raised the rifle, and glimpsed the long, tawny shape that flashed through the dark green of the trees, coming at him in long, low, swerving bounds. "Dammit," he swore aloud as he fired. He knew his shot was too hasty as the cougar sprang from the trees at him. He fired another shot and saw it go wild as his feet went out from under him, and he fell, sliding helplessly down the steep, narrow path. He slammed into Dawn, and she went down half atop him as he slid past her. The rifle fell from his hands as he reached out to try and grab hold of a shrub to slow his fall, but he caught hold of one only to feel it tear from his grasp.

Dawn was sliding down just above him, and he heard the cougar in the trees on the other side now, the big cat keeping pace with them, waiting to find the right spot to leap again. But the bottom of the steep runoff was in sight, and as he half fell and half slid he managed to yank the Colt from its holster. As the steep path ended with him sprawled on his stomach and Dawn sliding down beside him, he raised the Colt, squinted, caught a flash of movement in the trees, and fired four shots in a cluster. There was no howl or hiss of pain. None of them hit, but he heard the cougar racing away, bounding through the brush, and he breathed a deep sigh of relief.

He rose, crawled upward a half-dozen yards where the rifle had slid to a halt, and retrieved the gun. Dawn had pushed to her feet, the shock still stark in her eyes as he led the few yards onto the spot where the Ovaro still waited. He took a moment to reload the Colt before he climbed onto the horse with Dawn in the saddle in front of him. She leaned back as they rode, and he could feel the dejection inside her in the way she slumped against him. The night had come down to cloak the mountains when they reached her place, and she lighted the lamp as he unsaddled the pinto and put the horse behind the house with her gray mount. She was sitting, head bowed, by the table when he came back inside. "How about some of that applejack?" he suggested.

"Yes," she said with a nod. "That would be nice." She went to the small cabinet and brought out the crock and poured a glass for herself and him. "No toasts, please," she said as she took a deep pull of her drink.

"No toasts," he agreed and sat beside her on the sofa.

She voiced the questions though she really didn't need to do so. They were there in her eyes as she stared at him. "What's happened, Fargo? Why, why?" she asked. "You came to me, made my life so new and wonderful, and now this. I don't understand it. It's as if I'm being punished for having found the wonderfulness you brought me."

"Punished isn't exactly the right word," he said. The thoughts had been forming themselves during the long ride back, but the right words still eluded him. Perhaps because these truths were not made of facts, rights, and wrongs, tangible elements one could grasp hold of simply hold up to view. These truths were made of concepts he found hard to define, realizations that went far beyond the ordinary awareness of most people. These were truths made for philsophers and poets and those who speculated about the human condition. Yet they were as real as any hard-fact truths. He was witness to that, and, in a way, he had found proof of feelings he had always held in an undefined, amorphous manner. A preacher man had once told him that there were people, who by their very special qualities, manage to show the rest of us the inner truths of our existence. In her own way, Dawn was one of those people, he realized as he met her waiting, round gaze. Only it was clear now that she had always been as much pupil as teacher and had been unaware of being either one.

He took a deep breath and was about to find words to begin when the sharp whinny sounded. He recognized the Ovaro first, and then heard Dawn's horse join in. "Goddamn," Fargo bit out as he leaped to his feet. "He's near. He trailed us back." Dawn stared at him, her lips parted. "Stay here," he said and ran from the house, the Colt in his hand. He paused outside to scan the deep black circle of trees that surrounded the house. He listened, heard nothing, and edged his way with his back against the outside wall of the house. He reached the rear, calmed the two horses, and dropped the Colt back into its holster as he drew the rifle from its sheath against the saddle on the ground.

He moved back along the house again, his eyes peering at the blackness. The damn cougar was out there, watching, he knew. The sudden terror of the two horses had foiled its attempt to lurk unsuspected and silent. In cougar fashion, it would most likely wait till dawn before striking, but they were unpredictable. It could decide to go for the horses, and he didn't want that. "I'm going to stay out here for the night," he told Dawn as she came to the door.

"I'll stay with you," she said.

"No. I want him to have as few targets as possible," Fargo said. "You stay inside and keep the door closed."

"Be careful," she said as she clung to him for a moment and then stepped back and shut the door. He turned at once, listened, and again made his way to where the horses were tethered. The cougar was out there—the nervousness of the horses were proof of it—and Fargo sank to the ground with his back against the rear wall of the house. Trying to peer into the blackness of the trees was a waste of time, and he let his ears become his eyes. But the big cat was silent, and he heard nothing as the hours wore on. The moon slowly made its trackless path across the sky, and Fargo rose, stretched his cramped leg muscles for a moment, and then sank down to the ground again.

If the cougar did decide to attack in the night, he'd still have to come across the cleared stretch of ground between the trees and the front of the house. Fargo estimated he'd have thirty seconds at most to fire. Enough time for him, even in the dim moonlight. The most dangerous time would be when the moon sank over the high peaks. It would be pitch black then, the hanging hour before the sun rose. If the cougar charged then he'd be in real trouble, the cat's night vision being far superior to his. He could only hope the cougar stayed to form and obeyed its normal dislike of attacking in the blackness of night.

Fargo forced himself to relax. He knew Dawn lay awake inside the house, and he felt for her. That kind of waiting was even harder. She had nothing to cling to but helplessness and hope. He at least had the tension of the moment, the feel of the gun in his hand, and the waiting to strike for himself. As the night drew to an end and the moon began to drop behind the high mountains, the utter silence continued. There had been nothing but silence from the blackness of the trees, but then the cougar could prowl with total soundlessness. Yet he could almost believe the hunter had broken off the hunt and left.

Only the continued nervousness of the two horses told him this wasn't so.

His presence with them had a calming effect, but their ears still twitched constantly, and they moved back and forth restlessly against their tethers. The damn cat was out there. He grimaced and took a firmer grip on the big Sharps. He moved away from the horses and the rear of the house to position himself at the corner where he would command a clear view of the side and front where the line of trees faced the house. He waited, his ears straining, and he knew a thin line of perspiration had formed on his brow. He stared across the small cleared space as the pitch blackness began to slowly lighten. Dawn edged its way up and over the high peaks, and the blackness turned lighter, became deep gray, then light gray. He could see the trees now, silent and unmoving, and he rose to rest on one knee, the rifle almost at his shoulder. He swept the tree line with his eyes, back and forth, from one end to the other, and the first pink streaks of the new day touched the sky.

His eyes were still scanning the trees when he heard the sound—the creak of a tree branch behind the house and then the soft, thudding sound. "Dammit," he spit out as he leaped to his feet and ran under the overhang at the rear of the house. The rear corner of the house was obviously close enough to one of the big spruces. The soft thud had drawn the picture instantly. The cougar had climbed the tree, waited in the branches for enough light to spread over the scene, and then leaped down onto the roof with one powerful bound. Fargo moved under the overhang, ran his hands down the Ovaro and the gray horse. Both were very nervous now, aware that the cougar was close.

The damn cat had even more of an advantage now, Fargo realized bitterly. Dawn had to have heard the thud on the roof, and she knew at once what it meant. Now the cougar held her hostage inside the house and him hostage outside. All it had to do was wait for its prey to move, and the cougar was a hunter that *knew* how to wait.

8

Fargo leaned against the wall of the house. He had to go over his options before he could make plans, and he found that took him but a few seconds. He had no options, he realized. All he had was to decide what not to do. The cougar had all the options. It could leave as silently as it had come. It could decide to wait in the deep of the forest again. It could wait on the roof, knowing that waiting was on its side. Or it could silently drop to the ground on the opposite side and crash through a window into the house. He could never get into the house fast enough to save Dawn, Fargo knew, and the thought sent a stab of coldness through him. Or, the big cat could try to trigger a mistake. If it was that cunning, and he had the grim feeling that it was.

He snapped away his despairing thoughts and stepped a few paces to the edge of the overhang to peer upward, the rifle raised to fire. But he saw nothing. The mountain lion was staying back from the edge of the roof, and Fargo ducked back under the overhang. His eyes were narrowed as he peered into the clear land in front of the house, now bathed in the brightness of the sun. He let possibilities move through his thoughts, seeing mind pictures as he did, measuring steps, even twisting his body in a kind of mock rehearsal. He'd race into the open, and the cougar would see him at once, take one long bound across the roof and a second leap through the air. Fargo saw himself as he skidded to a halt, whirled, brought the rifle up, and fired.

He had counted off twenty seconds for himself, if everything went perfectly, if he didn't slip when whirling, if his first shot was on target. If he slipped or missed with the first shot he added another five seconds. Twenty or twenty-five, he repeated and then let himself follow the cougar's movements. He counted off the seconds as the big cat made its first bound across the roof and then leaped through the air at him. Twelve seconds, he cursed, too fast for him to get the rifle up and fire. Perhaps he could cut ten seconds from his time, he muttered and knew it was but an empty thought.

Dawn's voice broke into his thoughts, faint from inside the house. "Fargo," she called. "Are you all right? Can you hear me?"

"I'm fine," he called out.

"I haven't slept all night," Dawn called back. "Maybe if I came out you'd have a chance at it."

"No. Too risky," he said. "You stay inside. I'll think of something," he added with more confidence than he felt. She said nothing more, and he leaned back against the house again. He'd only had a few minutes of fruitless thought when he heard the cougar move, and he stepped forward and listened. The big cat was pacing up and down on the roof, no silent, stealthy steps now, but each pace a deliberate, scraping sound as it raked its long claws across the roof. Back and forth it moved, along the center of the roof, out of his sight, back and forth. Only an hour had passed, and Fargo felt his nerves beginning to tear at the constant, menacing pacing, each claw scrape an increasingly ominous sound.

His lips drew back as he knew what the sound must be to Dawn inside the house when suddenly the big cat stopped pacing, and Fargo heard the tearing, ripping sounds. The cougar had begun to tear into the old wood of the roof, its powerful forepaws pulling up long strips with each raking motion. It increased the fury of its digging, and Fargo could hear the old, weathered wood being gouged and ripped up. Goddammit, Fargo swore. It was tearing a hole in the roof, making progress too swiftly. But a small hole would not let it enter, Fargo knew. It would have to tear up more of the roof, and even as he said it he knew the prospect was all too possible.

Then, as suddenly as it had begun to rip a hole in the roof, the cougar stopped and began to pace again with its deliberate, scraping steps. It continued its slow, maddening pacing without a stop as another hour went by, and suddenly Dawn's voice came to him. "Fargo, I can't stand it. I've got to get out of here," she cried out, and he heard the near edge of hysteria in her voice.

"No, stay there," Fargo shouted back, and he ran from beneath the overhang, yanking the Colt from his pocket. He halted and emptied the Colt into the roof as he held the rifle in his other hand. The cougar stopped pacing as the shots filled the air, and moments after they died away it began to pace again. It had added disdain to its nerve-shattering pacing, and Fargo returned to the overhang to reload the Colt and push it back into the holster. He cast an eye at the Ovaro and Dawn's horse and wondered how long their nerves would last before they broke their tethers and fled. He cast a glance out into the clear land and saw the sun's shadows had grown longer. But there was still at least two hours of daylight left. If they could hold out till night, perhaps the moonlight would be the best chance. It would add another burden on sharpshooting at a fast-moving flash of a target, but he had hit the mark before under the moon's pale light.

Once again the cougar interrupted his thoughts as it stopped pacing and began to tear at the roof again, both powerful forepaws ripping and gouging. Another hour went by as it kept up its furious tearing. From the depth of its own instinctual wisdom it knew the value of mounting tension. It knew the way to shatter its prey's nerves so that it bounded into the path of swift death. Fargo cursed as he heard a piece of wood torn up, then another and another, an unceasing pressure, and suddenly the ripping sound stopped, and it was Dawn's scream that came.

"Oh, God, it's torn a hole through. It's staring down at me," she cried out. Fargo heard the cougar's snarl, a guttural promise of death. "I can't stand it. I can't stand it," Dawn screamed.

"Don't run. Stay there. Hold on a little longer. It can't get at you, not yet, not till it makes more of a hole," Fargo called back. He had just finished his pleas when he heard the ripping sound of a large piece of wood being torn away. He realized at once what had happened. With the first hole made, the cougar was able to get his claws around the end of a piece of wood and bring all its power to bear.

"Oh, no, no . . oh, no," Fargo heard Dawn scream, and seconds later he heard the front door of the house fly open. He spun and lifted the rifle as she raced from the house, running across the open land in terror and panic. Fargo ran forward into the open, dropped to one knee, and brought the rifle up to the edge of the roof at the front of the house, waited for the great, tawny form to leap into the dusk air. But the cougar didn't materialize in his sights, and suddenly he heard the rush of air. He half turned and saw the big cat flying through the air at him. It had outwitted him. It hadn't gone after Dawn, aware it could hunt her down at its leisure. Fargo knew he had no time to bring the rifle up and around, and he threw himself flat and felt the cougar's claw rip through his shirt. He rolled, not attempting to regain his feet, and swept the rifle around as he lay on his stomach. He saw the cougar land on all four feet, spin, and come at him, huge yellowed fangs bared.

Fargo fired from his prone position, point-blank at the yellow-eyed fury that was hardly more than a few feet from him. He rolled again the instant he got off the first shot and came up on his stomach again to fire once more, but he saw the cougar's forelegs crumple and the long, sleek body pitch forward. The big cat gave a last guttural snarl, twitched, and lay still. Fargo rose to his feet, and his mouth felt as though it were stuffed with cotton as he walked to the still form, being careful, approaching it from the rear. But as he halted beside it he saw that his point-blank shot had blown the great head into smithereens.

He felt the breath drain from him in a long sigh. If the shot had missed, he would be the one lying lifeless and torn apart in the same spot. He lifted his eyes to peer across the ground, the dusk moving down quickly, and at the edge of the trees he saw the yellow-haired, long figure standing. He raised an arm, and Dawn moved toward him, slow, deliberate steps until she neared him, and then she flew against him, and he felt the quivering of her. His arm around her waist, he walked into the house with her, and she lowered herself onto the sofa. The hole in the roof was a few feet to the right, he saw, a silent, grim reminder of what might have been. He set the rifle down and poured a glass of the applejack for her and for himself and edged down beside her.

She drank deeply of hers, took another long pull, and her eyes found his, the same questions in their light blue orbs as before the cougar had returned. "Why? What happened? What went so wrong suddenly?" Dawn asked.

"Nothing went wrong. Something changed," he said.

"I'm not being punished, you said. What, then?" she questioned. "What changed?"

"You," he said, and the tiny furrow touched her brow.

"By finding a new wonderfulness with you?" she asked. "By feeling more whole, more alive than I ever felt before?" He nodded, and she frowned back. "No, that's not right. It can't be," she said.

"But it is," he said and took her hand in his as suddenly she seemed the little girl again. "You gained something, and you lost something. Part of you grew, for always, and part of you left, forever. Finding and losing."

Her eyes stayed wide. "What did I find?" she asked.

"You found a part of you that waited to be discovered, that had to be discovered someday. You found a new power, a new secret, a new glory. You found the woman waiting inside you."

"And what did I lose?"

"Purity. Innocence. A kind of trust that will never be yours again," he said.

"I don't know that I like that," she frowned.

"That's how it happens, like it or not," he said gently.

"And the animals, the birds, all of them, they understood that when I didn't?" she questioned.

"They didn't understand it, but they felt it, sensed it, knew it as surely as they knew the you that was," he said.

"And was no longer," she murmured.

"That's right. You had changed. Instinct told them that. You were different. You could no longer be in tune with them the way you once were."

"There's something very sad here," Dawn said with a frown.

"That's as good a word as any, but it's never been different. Some call it simply growing up, but it all means changing."

"Why can't it all be one, the before and the after? Why must the new me change the old me? Why must the wonderful things I found change what I was? Why can't purity and growing up be a part of each other? Why can't they stay together?" She flung the questions at him in an explosion of protest.

He felt the ruefulness in his smile. "You want answers I'm not sure anyone can give you. I know for sure I can't," he said. "That's just the way of it, always has been. Maybe you're right. Maybe it shouldn't be that way. But it is."

She looked into space for a long moment before she spoke again. "Remember I told you I believed everything happens for a reason? Maybe the time had come for me to change. Maybe that's why you came my way. Maybe that's why I went out to let you find me."

"Maybe," he said. "But you know what else this

means, don't you?" he asked, and she waited. "You can't stay up here alone, the way you have been."

Her frown was instant. "You mean leave? I love it here, and I've so much work to do yet, so many drawings yet to make."

"You loved it the way it was. It's all different now. That doesn't mean you can't come back again, but not all alone. You'll have to make different arrangements, bring someone to help," he told her.

"You mean a friend?" she asked.

"Friend, husband, lover, someone you'll be comfortable with."

"I've been comfortable alone."

"Yes, but you're not part of the mountain now, not as you were. You were part of the wild creatures, and that gave you a special place. You can still be their friend, but you'll always be an outsider now," he said.

The night had fallen, and they were sitting in almost pitch blackness. She rose and turned the lamp on low. "It's all so new so suddenly. I have to think more," she said, and she rose and closed the door. He smiled to himself. Her thinking was already done. She just didn't know it. Little gestures, the signs we don't recognize ourselves.

"Do you have anywhere to go?" he asked.

"I've an aunt in Wallowa," she said.

"That's in Oregon Territory," he said, and she nodded.

"My father, always a practical man, left a trust fund for me with her, just in case something should happen to him. It's there waiting for me," she said.

"I'll take you there," he said.

"I said I'll have to think more on it," she answered with some stiffness in her voice. "Come inside with me now," she said, reaching out to him, and he rose and followed her into the bedroom. He shed his clothes, and she pulled the dress off and folded herself in his arms.

"You feeling sorry for all this?" he asked. "You want to turn back the clock?"

"How can I want that when all I want is you with me, kissing me, touching me, taking me?" she said. "Make me forget today, Fargo."

"Can't do that," he said. "I can make you not think about it for tonight."

"I'll settle for that," she said, and her hand crept down to find his warmth already beginning to throb. He was gentle with her wood-sprite loveliness, especially gentle, and she was especially wanting, and finally she slept against him, satiated and content. He lay awake, thinking of all the questions she'd thrown at him, and he wondered if anyone, anywhere, anytime, would have answers for them. He slept finally and woke with the new sun, quietly slid from the bed without waking Dawn, and pulled on his trousers. He hurried outside and dragged the body of the cougar into the trees. He wanted it out of the way before the buzzards found it, but mostly so Dawn wouldn't see it when she came out.

She had mentally accepted the things he'd told her, acceding to the truth of her new position here. Yet her caring and devotion to the mountain creatures hadn't diminished. That would never leave, he knew, and seeing the once-great tawny form would only add more pain, and she had more than enough of that to absorb. She was at the well, washing, when he emerged from the trees. Her wood-nymph loveliness gave him a moment of doubt as he wondered if he was uprooting something that did indeed belong here. He hurried to her, handed her the towel she'd put on the ground, and her eyes were serious as they turned to him.

"I've done my thinking," she said.

"I'll help you get your things together," he said, and she frowned.

"How do you know that's what I decided?" she questioned with a protest in her voice.

"Doors," he chuckled, and her frown continued to question. "When some folks close them it doesn't mean much. When others do it means everything," he said. She sniffed and followed him into the house where he began to help her collect the things she wanted to take, mostly clothes, her rifle, and all her drawings which were inside a large sketchpad. She surprised him by dragging a saddle from under the bed.

"I'd rather ride bareback, but I can hang things from it," she said grudgingly. He put the saddle on the gray horse, hung her travel bags from the saddle horn, and tied her drawing to the saddle string from the rear skirt. He saw the pain in her eyes as she rode beside him. She rode stiffly, refusing to look back. He didn't try to comfort her with words. She didn't deserve that. She had earned her right to her own pain. Growing up was more than losing innocence and purity.

The mountainsides grew steep and demanded his concentration, and he saw Dawn had more difficulty clinging to the saddle than she had riding bareback. They had reached a spot where the steepness leveled off, and she came alongside him as he took a trail that cut between two ridges. He had cast a glance at her when the movement on the ridge caught his eye, and he peered upward at the line of juniper. He saw the movement again, and it took shape, became a horse and rider, followed by another and still another, all moving single file along the ridge. His glance went to the other ridge, and he saw another line of horsemen and caught the flash of bronze skin in a glint of sunlight.

"We've company," he said to Dawn, and she glanced at the ridge nearest her. "Shoshoni," he muttered.

"But I thought . . ." she began.

"That they were afraid to come near you?" he finished.

"Yes. That's what happened at the camp," Dawn said.

"That was then," Fargo said, and she frowned at him. "The spirit woman has gone, lost her powers," he said. "No more magical qualities."

"How do they know I've changed? They didn't see what happened with the cougar or the eagle or the deer," Dawn said. "Are you telling me they're as sensitive as the deer and the foxes, that they just know I've changed?"

"No, it wasn't instinct with them. They just put two-and-two together," Fargo said.

"I don't understand."

"You came to their camp, and they ran. You were the spirit woman. If Gibson and his men had been there when they got back, they wouldn't be here after us now. But Gibson was gone, all of their prisoners gone."

"I had released their prisoners. I was no longer someone of magical powers, apart from everyone else. I was just one more enemy," Dawn said.

"Bull's-eye," Fargo said.

"They took a different road to the same place," Dawn said, and he heard the wryness in her words.

His eyes were narrowed as he peered ahead. The two ridges stayed parallel to the passage where they rode, the tree cover heavier. They'd be forced to go more slowly, and they'd lose more time when they left the ridges to go down the brush-covered slopes.

"We're going to have to find a place to make a stand," he told Dawn. "But first we've got to make some time on them. You ready to ride?" She nodded, and he dug his heels into the Ovaro's ribs, and the horse went into an instant gallop. He saw Dawn start after him, flicked a glance up at the ridge to his right, and saw the Shoshoni hadn't reacted yet. They'd have lost almost a minute by the time they did, he grunted in satisfaction as he sent the Ovaro charging down the passage. He glanced back to see Dawn was a dozen yards behind, but not losing any further ground.

The passage began to narrow, he saw, and another glance upward showed the Shoshoni were riding hard now, but losing ground in the dense tree cover. They'd swerve down from the two ridges in another minute and fall back further in the process, but they knew their quarry would outrun them if they didn't. Dawn's quarter horse kept its pace, Fargo saw, and he concentrated on the terrain ahead as the passage continued to narrow. He galloped another few hundred yards when he saw the passage narrow to where only a single horse and rider could follow at a time. The sides rose up steeply, but he spotted a place where rain runoff had dug ruts on both sides of the steep slopes. He reined to a halt. "You take that side," he said, pointing to the left rut. "I'll take this one. We pick them off as they come through."

"I can't," she said. "I can't shoot a human being."

"You told me you'd killed game to survive," he said.

"That was to survive," she said.

"So's this, honey," he flung back as he sent the Ovaro up the rut in the steep slope to his right. The Shoshoni hadn't come into sight yet behind them. "Move, dammit," he barked, and she sent the horse up the rut on the other side. He halted a dozen yards up the slope, leaped from the horse with the big Sharps in hand, and peered across to the opposite slope to see Dawn halt and slide from the gray, her rifle held at her side. She was looking across at him, he saw, and he hunkered down behind a spruce. She had just done the same when he heard the Shoshoni coming, riding hard. He raised the rifle to his shoulder.

The first Indian came by, the one with the bear claw in his ear. Fargo let him pass, let two more go by until there were at least six in the narrow passage below. He fired, then, fast, on-target shots that sent three of the Shoshoni toppling. He swung the rifle to find the leader and saw that the Indian had leaped from his pony as the horse ran on. The brave just behind him dived from his mount as Fargo's shot grazed his scalp. He brought the rifle back to where four more Shoshoni were streaking through the narrowest part of the passage. Dawn still hadn't fired, he cursed as he let go another round of shots, and two more racing horsemen fell. But two raced through and out of sight, and Fargo saw the last four Indians enter the passage when the first one skidded his pony to a halt as Fargo's shot whistled past his head.

"Fire, dammit, fire," he shouted as there was still no rifle shot from the other side of the passage. The last four Shoshoni were managing to turn their ponies in the narrowness of the passage to race back rather than run the gauntlet of fire. Only there was no gauntlet, Fargo swore. There was only him, and he yanked the Colt out to use the speed of the six-gun as the last four braves were racing out of the passage. He had the satisfaction of seeing two go down before the first two disappeared from sight. "Damn you, girl," he shouted, realizing that he'd let anger and disappointment get the better of caution as his ears caught the swish of air.

He half turned and tried to duck, but the tomahawk caught him on the arm, a grazing blow, but enough to send the Colt flying from his hand. He fell forward, his arm instantly numb as he saw the Shoshoni move toward him down the slope, the bear claw in his earlobe and the hunting knife in his hand. The Indian had climbed up the slope after diving from his horse, and he circled back. Fargo cursed silently as he turned to meet the man's leap. The Shoshoni came down, the knife raised to plunge it forward, but Fargo didn't try to parry the blow. Instead, he flung himself flat, and the Shoshoni fell forward past him, landed on his hands and knees and spun around.

He rose, came forward again, and Fargo backed along the slope and cursed the numbness still seizing his arm. He let the Indian come at him, waited, saw the man's feet dig into the soil, and was ready for the diving leap. Fargo kicked out, his foot smashing into the Shoshoni's midsection. The Indian let out a gasp of pain as he doubled over. Fargo used his left to bring up a sharp hook that landed on the Indian's jaw, and the man fell backward down the slope. Fargo leaped after him, but slowed as he saw the Indian still clutched the knife. He stepped sideways as the Shoshoni started to regain his feet and kicked out again, this time his blow sinking into the man's ribs, and once again the Indian went down as he lost his balance on the slope.

Fargo felt the numbness in his arm beginning to lessen as he came forward again. The Shoshoni, pulling himself to one knee, sent the knife sweeping out in an arc, and Fargo just managed to pull his legs back as the blow grazed his calves. He dived, landed atop the Indian, rolled with him, and closed one hand around the man's knife hand. He was atop the Shoshoni, pressing down on the man's neck with his knee while he clung to the knife hand, when he felt the blow come down on the back of his head. The sharp pain shot through him, and he rolled away, the world going gray. He shook his head and the grayness lifted, but the pain stayed. He glimpsed the second Shoshoni who had come from behind to strike him, the tomahawk still in the man's hand.

Fargo winced in pain as a kick slammed into his side, rolling him a half-dozen feet down the slope, and he saw the brave with the bear claw coming after him. Both Shoshoni seized him, yanked him to his feet, and the one sunk a blow into his stomach that dropped him to the ground again. Fighting away the pain in his head and stomach, he wrapped his arms around the nearest pair of legs and pulled, and one of the men went down with a roar of surprise more than pain. Fargo didn't leap on him, but instead rolled aside and felt the other Indian's tomahawk graze his shoulder. With a snarl of surprise, the brave spun and charged at him as Fargo got to one knee. He saw the short-handled ax come down at him and managed to twist his body. He felt the weapon skitter along his shoulder blade instead of splitting his skull open.

He wrapped both arms around the Indian's knees and dove forward, taking the man down with him. He started to bring his arm around in a swinging blow when the kick caught him on the back of his head and he fell sideways. The world turned gray again, stayed that way for uncounted moments, and when the grayness lifted he was on his back, both Shoshoni standing over him, a foot pressing each of his wrists into the ground. He peered up at the figures through eyes that were still haze, but he saw the one held the knife, the other the tomahawk. He blinked, and the haze cleared. He'd have a good, sharp view of his death, he realized with bitter irony as the one Indian raised the knife, the other his tomahawk.

"The woman," one said. "Where is the woman?"

"Goddamn good question," Fargo said. He knew they didn't understand him, but they understood he'd given them no answer. With a half-roar of fury and triumph they started to bring their weapons down. The two explosions of sound seemed unreal as the two Shoshoni suddenly quivered, their bodies buckling. They seemed to do a slow rigadoon as they half turned toward each other with their bodies still buckled, and then as they sank to the ground he saw the redness gushing from their backs. He pulled his arms down, skidded himself backward and looked up to see the figure standing on the slope, the rifle in her hands, yellow cornsilk hair falling to one side of her face.

"It took you long enough," he muttered as he pushed to his feet. "You didn't fire one shot at them in the passage, dammit," he said.

"I know," she said quietly. "I couldn't."

"What made you do it just now?" he questioned.

"Survival. Your survival," she said.

He drew a long breath. "Better late than never," he said and drew her to him. She stayed against him in silence, and he finally stepped back, retrieved the

Colt and the rifle, and led her down the slope as the pinto followed. Her horse waited in the passage, and he helped her climb into the saddle and led the way past the bodies of the slain Shoshoni until they were moving down the mountainside once again. She rode in silence beside him until the day began to end, and he found a place to bed down beneath a circle of Hawthorn.

"When we left the house I told myself I'd come back someday," she said. "Now I don't think I will."

"Why not?" he asked.

"It's all changed, too much changed," she said.

"Has it?" he smiled.

Her smile was a rueful echo. "No, I've changed. I could never see it with the same eyes again. I never knew how much things are what we bring to them."

"You've learned something most folks never learn," he told her.

"I want always to remember two things," she said. "The time that once was and the time that was with you."

"Fair enough," he said, and she came to him on the bedroll, to him, for him, and with him, and when she lay asleep in his arms he wondered which he would remember the longest, the girl-woman or the woman-girl. Perhaps they'd never be entirely separate, not for him and, he hoped, not for her.

LOOKING FORWARD!
The following is the opening
section from the next novel in the exicting
Trailsman series from Signet:

THE TRAILSMAN #135
MONTANA MAYHEM

Spring, 1859—the Swan Range
of the Rockies, where unwary whites
often fell prey to bloodthirsty
Blackfoot, savage beasts,
or their own brutal lust . . .

Skye Fargo frowned when he heard the shot.

A big man who moved with the fluid ease of a prowling mountain lion, he paused in a stand of pines on the west slope of a jagged peak and cocked his head to listen for a second report. The shot had come from below and to the north, perhaps a quarter of a mile off. It meant there were others in the area, and because he was in a remote region seldom penetrated by whites, those others must be Indians.

He glanced down at the fresh elk tracks he had been following, his frown deepening. His hope of a succulent steak for supper was now shattered. if he fired his Sharps, he risked having the shot heard by the Indians. And the last thing he wanted was to tangle with a war party of Bannock or Blackfoot.

Annoyed, he pivoted and headed down the slope. It would be best to pack up, saddle the Ovaro, and get the hell out of there before the Indians stumbled on his camp. He would ride farther west, being careful to skirt Flathead Lake, and enter territory where even the neighboring tribes rarely ventured.

All Fargo wanted was to be left alone so he could hunt, fish, and trap in peace for two or three weeks. In recent months he had spent more time than was his custom in various towns and cities scattered from the Mississippi River to the Pacific Ocean, and he was tired of being among crowds of people. A loner at heart, he had had his fill of civilization for a while.

The old, familiar longing had returned on a visit to Denver, a longing for the wilderness he called his home, for the wideopen spaces where a man could live as he pleased without interference from another living soul. So he had bought extra supplies and ridden north until he reached Fort Benton. From there he had traveled westward into an isolated range of the majestic Rockies where he wouldn't encounter anyone else.

Or so he had thought.

He'd known, of course, that the Blackfoot, Assiniboin, Atsina, and Crow lived on the plains to the east. And that the Bannock, Kalispel, Shoshoni, and others all frequented the territory to the west and south. But the range he'd selected was so far off the beaten path, even for the Indians, that he'd figured on enjoying several weeks of uninterrupted solitude.

Sighing in frustration, Fargo hurried, his muscles rippling with latent power. His camp lay a half mile distant, and he feared the Indians might discover it before he got there. Losing his gear was of no consequence, but he couldn't abide the thought of losing his reliable pinto stallion. That horse had saved his hide more times than he cared to count, had carried him across blistering deserts and frigid prairies covered by deep snow, had taken him from one end of the country to the other and never once given him cause to complain. In a sense, the Ovaro was more like a friend than a dumb beast of burden, and he wasn't about to let it be stolen.

Suddenly more shots split the crisp mountain air, arising from the same direction. There were two quick blasts, followed by a half-dozen slightly fainter reports.

Fargo paused again. Those first two had been rifle shots, the others all made by pistols. Which might mean there were white men involved, since Indians rarely used revolvers. But what would a party of whites be doing in the area? The fur trade had long since died out, and except for a few grizzled diehards who trapped ranges much farther west where beaver were still abundant, the Rockies had seen their last of the wild and wooly trapping fraternity. Prospectors generally confined their activities far to the south near Denver, where gold had recently been discovered. And the nearest settlement was Fort Benton, over one hundred and thirty miles to the east. There was simply no reason for any white man to enter the region Skye was in, which was one of the reasons he had picked it.

Four more pistol shots.

Fargo firmed his grip on the heavy Sharps and broke into a dog trot. As tirelessly as an Apache, he had covered almost the entire half-mile when a hint of movement and a glimmer of bright color off to his right drew him up short behind the trunk of a spruce. Automatically he crouched and cocked the rifle, seeking the source of the movement. He saw her right away.

A redhead burst from cover at the opposite end of a meadow bordering the trees. Her hair flying, her features a study in determination, she pumped her limbs furiously, her yellow dress swirling about her shapely legs, her ample bosom heaving from her exertion. Twenty yards she went before she cast a hasty glance over her left shoulder, stumbled in a rut, and fell to one knee.

Fargo was about to step into the open to go to her aid when two men appeared. Both were grungy characters in shabby clothes. Both held pistols, and both were smirking as they closed in on their red-headed quarry.

The woman cried out, heaved upright, and resumed running for her life.

"Stop, missy!" bellowed the taller of the duo.

Ignoring him, the redhead raced like a frightened fawn toward the shelter of the forest.

"Stop, damn you!" the man barked, and snapped off a shot from the hip. The gun spat lead and smoke, the slug kicking up dirt beside her. "The next one will be in your leg," he warned.

With evident reluctance the woman finally halted. Her shoulders slumping, breathing heavily, she turned. "Why are you doing this?" she called out. "What do you want?"

Neither man answered until they were almost to

her, then the tall one laughed and raked his hungry gaze from her luxurious hair to her thighs. "What kind of a stupid question is that, missy? You know damn well what we want."

Fargo couldn't see her face, but he noticed her backbone stiffen and admired her gumption when she spoke.

"Yes, I suppose I do. Anyone who rides with Snake Haddock has to be vermin just like him. Haddock wouldn't know how to treat a decent woman if his life depended on it."

"We'll let you tell him that in person when he shows up later," the tall one responded with a sneer.

"Until then," said his companion, "you'd be wise to keep your pretty mouth shut."

"And what if I don't?" the woman defiantly replied.

Fargo tensed when the man backhanded her across the face. Rage welled up within him. Any man who would beat a defenseless woman deserved to be stomped into the ground. She staggered but kept her footing; then she was seized roughly by the tall hardcase and pulled northward. Fargo had seen enough! Rising, he sprinted in pursuit, staying shy of the meadow, staying among the trees where his buckskinclad frame was less likely to be spotted and where he could keep an eye on the redhead and her captors. They entered a tract of pines without once looking back.

Fargo didn't know what he was getting himself into, but he wasn't about to sit idly by and do nothing while the woman was hauled off against her will. He was tempted to shoot both men. Picking them off with the Sharps would be as easy as pie, but the shots were bound to be heard by any friends the pair might have in the vicinity. So it would be better to deal with them silently.

He probed the trees until he spied the woman's yellow dress, then poured on the speed until he was well ahead of the threesome. Slanting to a point directly in their path, he sought cover behind a fir tree, leaned the Sharps against the trunk, and slipped his right hand inside his boot to clasp his Arkansas toothpick. Voices told him the three were slowly approaching.

"—him what he wants to know or he'll have all of you killed," the tall one was saying. "Mark my words, missy. You don't want to get on the bad side of a man like Snake Haddock."

"I didn't know he had any other side," the woman replied sarcastically. "Are you sure we're talking about the same lying, thieving, back-shooting, no-account bastard?"

Fargo heard the tall man sigh. Peeking around the bole, he saw the three of them coming toward him. He guessed they would pass within six feet or so to his left.

"You're asking for grief, Agatha Jennings," the tall one declared. "If you get Snake all riled and he slits your throat, don't say I didn't warn you."

Easing onto his elbows and knees, Fargo scooted to the next tree, using weeds and a bush for cover. Uncoiling, he straightened and waited, scarcely breathing, girding himself for the moment they would come abreast of his hiding place.

"You're all heart, Murdock," the woman declared. "And here pa told me you're nothing but a low-down skunk."

"Hugh is a fine one to talk. He rode with us for two years, didn't he? He did more than his share of robbing and killing, I can tell you. So where does he get off acting so high and mighty now?"

"He quit. He's trying to reform."

The two hardcases laughed.

"You can't teach an old dog new tricks, missy," Murdock said. "If he told you he was giving up the old ways, he lied."

"Where is it?" the other man asked.

"Where is what?" Agatha responded.

The trio stepped into view, the redhead walking between her captors. Both men were staring at her. Both had returned their revolvers to their holsters.

Fargo launched himself from behind the trunk, reaching the tall one called Murdock in a single bound and pressing the razor tip of his knife against the man's throat before Murdock could react. "Give me any excuse and you're dead," he said, increasing the pressure to emphasize the point.

Murdock had frozen, his eyes wide in surprise.

The other man started to make a move for his six-shooter, then apparently thought better of the notion and stood still, his gun hand poised above his pistol. "Who are you, mister?" he demanded. "What the hell do you want?"

"I want you to pretend you're reaching for a pine cone," Fargo directed, and when the other man hesitated, he jabbed the toothpick a bit deeper into Murdock's flesh.

"Do as he says, Wolney!" Murdock declared. He gulped and blinked, glancing at Wolney out of the corner of his eye. "If you don't, and if this jasper doesn't kill me, I'll sure as blazes kill you!"

Wolney scowled but complied, extending both arms overhead. "You're making a big mistake, mister," he told Skye. "We ride with Snake Haddock. Give us trouble and you'll answer to him."

So far Agatha Jennings had not spoken a word. She was studying Fargo intently, her brow creased in deep thought, her hands on her slender hips.

"Take three steps straight backward, Miss Jennings," Skye instructed her. "I wouldn't want you to come between Wolney and me. He might get the hare-brained idea to go for that Remington on his hip, and then I'd have to kill both these gents."

Smiling ever so sweetly at her frustrated abductors, Agatha backed up a few feet. "Don't be bashful on my account, stranger," she said, addressing Fargo. "If you're inclined to rub these two out, have at it."

"Bitch!" Wolney snapped.

Fargo only had to shift his weight and lash out with his left boot to connect, his foot smashing into Wolney where it would do the most damage. Taken unawares, Wolney doubled over and clutched his groin, his face becoming beet red as he sputtered, gasped, and tottered. Fargo took a step rearward, being careful to hold the knife poised to slash should Murdock get any fancy ideas. Then, his body a blur, he planted a kick squarely on Wolney's jaw. The man dropped like a poled ox.

"Kick him again!" Agatha urged.

Ignoring her, Skye wagged the toothpick in Murdock's face. "How about you? Care to insult the lady?"

"Not me, mister. I know when to play a hand out and I know when to fold."

"Smart hombre," Fargo said, and deftly tossed the toothpick from his right hand to his left. In the blink of an eye he drew his Colt, training it on Murdock's chest. The click of the hammer sounded loud in the stillness of the forest. "Now unbuckle your gun belt and let it fall. No tricks or else."

"You don't have to tell me twice," Murdock said, using just one hand to unfasten his belt buckle. As his gun hit the earth he raised his arms, then nodded at the unconscious Wolney. "What are you fixing to do with us?"

"For starters, how about if I teach you some manners?" Fargo said sternly. "First lesson, don't go around hitting folks who can't fight back." With that he hauled off and clubbed Murdock across the face with the Colt barrel. The blow drove the tall man to his knees. Dazed, blood trickling from his nose, Murdock made a sluggish play for his gun. Fargo slugged him again. Down Murdock went, as limp as a wet rag.

Agatha Jennings laughed in delight. "You do know how to handle yourself, don't you, big fella?" she asked, coming forward and looping her arm over Fargo's left elbow.

"I saw them grab you," Fargo said, amused by the twinkle in her lovely green eyes and the frankly suggestive grin curling her rosy lips.

"I've always wanted a knight in shining armor to come to my rescue," Agatha said huskily, then started as if poked with a pin. "Oh, my God!" she blurted, pressing a hand to her mouth. Suddenly she started off through the pines, pulling him along with her.

"What am I thinking of! Pa and my sisters are in big trouble. You've got to help them, too."

"Whoa, there," Fargo said, trying to tug his arm from her clinging grasp. "What is this all about? I don't like to go into a bear's den unless I know what's in there."

"Four of Haddock's men jumped us," Agatha said. She jerked a thumb over her shoulder. "Those two will be out for hours, but the other two might have their grimy hands on the rest of my family by now. You have to help them."

"I have to do no such thing," Fargo countered. He dug in his heels, bringing both of them to a halt. "Not unless you tell me what's going on. Why are these men after you?"

"They're not after me, dunderhead," Agatha said impatiently. "They're after my pa."

"Why?"

"There's no time to explain, damn it!" Agatha said, hauling on his arm again. "If we don't hurry, it will be too late. My pa and my sisters will be killed and their blood will be on your hands!"

As if to prove her right, from several hundred yards to the north came the crack of a revolver, three times in swift succession.

"Please!" Agatha pleaded, tears forming as she frantically tried to get him to move. "Please don't let them die!"

"Oh, hell," Fargo muttered, and against his better judgment he let her lead him toward the shooting. He remembered the Sharps and almost stopped, but a strident scream from up ahead made him realize he might be too late if he went back for the rifle. So he raced alongside Agatha Jennings until he glimpsed figures moving in a clearing. Grabbing her wrist, he darted to the right behind a pine tree.

"What are you doing?" she objected. "We're not there yet."

"We're close enough," Fargo whispered. "And keep your voice down unless you want Haddock's men to hear you." He leaned out and scanned the clearing, which was situated at the base of a cliff flanking a high hill. Haddock's men were easy to spot; they were holding revolvers on a grizzled man in dirty long johns who was kneeling between them. Nearby stood two young women, a very attractive pair in their early twenties or thereabouts, both brunettes, one thin with hair to her shoulders and the other sporting thick hair down to her thighs. They appeared terrified. The man in the long johns was wringing his hands and glancing from one gunman to the other. He was saying something, but Skye couldn't make out the words.

"Do something!" Agatha goaded. "They'll kill him at any moment!"

"Hold your horses," Fargo muttered, trying to come up with a plan to distract Haddock's men so he could get the drop on them. It would be less of a headache to simply shoot them, but he wanted to learn what Snake Haddock was after, and they might be persuaded to tell him. The name Haddock had come up a few times in his travels, always in connection with one grisly crime or another. If Agatha's pa had been a member of the outlaw gang that rode with Haddock, then old man Jennings had to have a heart as black as the ace of spades. And what did that say about his daughters? "I want you to run around to the east side of the clearing. Stay hidden until you see me wave, then step into the open."

"And do what?"

"Nothing. Just stand there."

Agatha looked at him as if he was out of his mind. "Are you sure you know what you're doing? I don't want to get myself killed."

"I need an edge," Fargo informed her. "If I pop out of nowhere, they might start shooting and your family could get caught in the cross fire. Do you want that to happen?"

"No. Of course not. But what good will showing myself to them do?"

"It will buy me a second or two," Fargo said testily, annoyed at having his judgment questioned. "Don't worry about your hide. They want you alive, or Murdock and Wolney would have shot you."

She gazed toward the clearing and nodded. "Oh. Now I understand."

"And remember to keep your eyes on me until you're in position. I'll be making my way closer."

"You do know what you're doing," Agatha said, and smirked. Impulsively she pressed her body to his and gave him a kiss on the cheek, her soft, moist lips clinging to his skin for an instant before she dashed off to do his bidding.

Fargo watched her, admiring the lush curves that hinted at delights beyond measure. If he was any judge of women, Agatha Jennings would be a wildcat in bed. He put such thoughts aside at a sharp cry from the clearing.

One of Haddock's men had slugged Jennings, and the old man was now lying on his side, rubbing his jaw. The daughter with the long hair, her fists clenched, wanted to tear into the culprit but was being held back by her sister.

Skye padded nearer, exercising all his wilderness savvy, moving as stealthily as an Indian, pausing once to stick the throwing knife into its sheath inside his boot. He kept close track of Agatha, worried the two outlaws would spot her yellow dress. But they never so much as glanced at the forest. All they were concerned about was her father.

Why had Snake Haddock sent them? What did Haddock care if a gang member decided to call it quits? The outlaw trail was brutally hard, what with the outlaws always being on the run, always having to look over their shoulders, never having a safe place to call home. Once their identities became known to the law, their days were numbered. The smart ones realized their mistake early and got out while they could. Most wound up with a fatal case of lead poisoning. A few, a very few, made a career of it and lived to old age. Jennings must be in his fifties, an old-timer by frontier standards, well past his prime. If he wanted to hang up his guns, why should Haddock mind?

Soon he could hear the conversation between Jennings and the hardcases.

"—what we came for, Hugh. Snake told us he wanted you alive, but he didn't say we couldn't break a few bones if we were of a mind," a beefy man in a black hat said.

"I don't know what you're talkin' about," Jennings responded. "Snake is loco if he thinks I did."

"The boss is a lot of things, but loco isn't one of them. If he says you did, you did."

Fargo reached a tree near the clearing and stopped. Agatha was to the east, expectantly staring at him. A flick of a hand was his signal, and she quickly edged closer to the open space. Neither of the outlaws noticed her until she walked a half-dozen feet from the trees. Then they both did and whirled, their revolvers leveled.

"Agatha!" the man in the black hat declared. "What are you doing back? I thought you were heading for the hills."

"I came to my senses, Dorn, and came back to be with my family," she answered, giving her father and sisters a reassuring smile.

"Where's Murdock and Wolney?" Dorn asked suspiciously.

"I gave those yacks the slip. Between the two of them, they don't have the brains God gave a turnip."

The gunmen laughed.

"Ain't that the truth!" Dorn said good-naturedly. "Why, Wolney is the dumbest critter this side of the Divide. Once we held up some miners and they showed their grit by fighting back. That fool Wolney drew his six-shooter and took to firing, but all the chambers were empty. He'd forgotten to reload his six-shooter the night before when he was cleaning it. About got himself killed."

By then Fargo had taken three long strides, his soles making no noise on the soft grass. He was a couple of yards from them when he halted and announced, "Howdy, gents. Don't make any sudden moves. I never forget to reload my gun." He saw them go rigid. Their backs were to him, so he couldn't see their faces, but he could tell by the tone of Dorn's reply that there would be gunplay.

"Who are you, mister? Why are you throwing a hand in this?"

"I'm the one who taught Murdock and Wolney some manners," Skye said in the hope these two wouldn't try anything if they knew their companions were out of commission. "And I'll do the same to you if you don't throw your hog-legs down right this minute."

Dorn snorted. "We're from Missouri, stranger."

With that, both gunmen whirled.